A bullet from a high-powered rifle snicked into the snow scarcely five feet from Sean.

Dodging and twisting, he raced back up the slope. Just before he broke over the crest of the hill, Sean heard the musical notes of a hunting horn. Almost at once the mournful bay of a trailing hound answered the summons.

Slasher—the murdering half-breed coyote— had been killing the hill men's stock and they were grimly out for revenge.

But it wasn't Slasher's trail the hounds were on. It was Sean's!

———

"Jim Kjelgaard, with his first-hand knowledge of Irish setters and the outdoors, has spun a fascinating tale. Definitely one of his finest."
—*Chicago Tribune*

Outlaw Red
by Jim Kjelgaard

A BANTAM SKYLARK BOOK®
TORONTO · NEW YORK · LONDON · SYDNEY · AUCKLAND

This edition contains the complete text
of the original hardcover edition.
NOT ONE WORD HAS BEEN OMITTED.

RL 4, 009–013

OUTLAW RED

*A Bantam Skylark Book / published by arrangement with
Holiday House, Inc.*

PRINTING HISTORY
Holiday House edition published September 1953
Bantam edition / September 1977
10 printings through August 1988

FOR
Carl and Bertha Kjelgaard

Contents

1. Show Dog

Sean, largest and handsomest of Champion Big Red's sons, was stretched full length in the wire cage that enclosed him. He seemed to be sleeping. But he was wide awake, his unblinking eyes fixed on a mouse that was creeping furtively from beneath his kennel. No muscle twitched in the Irish Setter's superb body and, in spite of the breeze, even Sean's hair did not blow. Almost he seemed to be dead.

The red dog's stillness was partly a masquerade, the result of long hours spent in inventing games that he could play, and partly a marvelous hunting inheritance.

Hundreds of years ago Irish Setters had been bred by discerning huntsmen of the Irish bogs. Born in them was the instinct to use their intelligence, and to react instantly to anything that might arise. Sean had inherited all this wisdom from his father, Big Red, who knew everything there was to know about the wilderness. Though Sean himself had seldom been in the surrounding Wintapi forests, his birthright was a knowledge of how to conduct himself as a hunter.

He knew that he must lie quietly now because, if he did not, the mouse would whisk back beneath the kennel and would not come out again. Still pretending to sleep, Sean remained wide awake, his eyes on the mouse.

So well did the red dog know the various things about his run that he could tell almost exactly what the mouse was going to do next. Two feet from the mouse's safe shelter under the kennel was a fleck of food that Sean, shaking his head after eating, had deposited there. Sean knew that the mouse wanted that tempting morsel. Unmoving, careful to do nothing that might cause alarm, he watched the tiny creature edge forward.

Stopping every inch to reconnoiter, the mouse came its own length from the bottom of the kennel. It was a very symbol of caution, a wild and much-harassed creature that had learned how to live in the midst of its enemies. Anything that moved was almost certain to mean danger.

The mouse moved six inches, constantly stopping to probe with every sense in its tiny body for an enemy that might be waiting. In the mouse's world, a wrong move meant death.

Sean watched and correctly interpreted every motion. He saw the mouse halt abruptly and knew that it had stopped because it was studying him. Sean scarcely breathed. This was one of the games that made his caged life bearable. He must do nothing to spoil it.

The mouse stood still, its only movement a nervous wriggling of its nose. Suddenly it flitted back toward the kennel.

Mischief glinted in Sean's deep-brown eyes, and he made a conscious effort to keep from running his pink tongue out in a happy grin. He knew what the mouse was doing. It had seen him, and, not knowing whether the big Setter was alive or not, was running to provoke Sean into betraying himself.

A moment later, having decided that Sean was harmless, the mouse went directly to the morsel of food and began to nibble. Still alert for enemies, but its wariness blunted by haste to finish the food before something else took it, the mouse ate rapidly. No longer could it wholeheartedly devote every sense to looking for enemies.

The second the mouse finished the food, Sean left the ground. Almost without effort, his graceful legs seeming to uncoil from his wonderful body, he went upward and outward. In a flurry of panic, the mouse turned to run.

The red-gold of Sean's body flashed in the sunlight, and reflected amber tints as the sun struck his fur. His ivory-fanged jaws, strong as a wolf's, opened and snapped shut a hair's breadth behind the fleeing mouse.

Sean snuffled under the kennel; the mouse had escaped him but not by very much. Then he relaxed in his run, an impish grin spreading his jaws. It had been great fun.

For a few minutes he padded idly about the run, inspecting all over again corners that he had investigated twice a thousand times. So long had he lived here, and so well did he know the place, that he was familiar with every strand of wire, every post, and even every nail and knothole in the posts and the few rust spots on the wire. He knew almost every clod of dirt and every paw print.

He liked none of it. The time he must spend in the

run was always a boring time. The brightest spot in his day was the hour when Billy Dash, the kennel boy, took him out for exercise.

Suddenly Sean walked eagerly to the end of his run and pushed his nose against the wire. His tongue lolled so that the pink tip protruded between his polished teeth, and his mouth formed a doggy smile. His brown eyes glinted with life, his ears were alert and his tail wagged happily back and forth. Another break had come in his monotonous day.

The meadow in which the kennels were built was part of a spacious valley. Forested mountains rose on either side, and at one end of the meadow a dirt road led down to the luxurious estate of Mr. Haggin, the wealthy man who owned the clearing, the kennels, all the dogs except Big Red, and the trim hunting lodge. Vaguely Sean recalled when there had been a rough mountaineer's cabin in place of the lodge, and a barn instead of kennels. At that time he had lived with his brother and three sisters in a crude pen made of chicken wire. Now the dogs lived in roomy kennels, while Danny Pickett and his father, Ross, who were in charge of the kennels, lived in the lodge.

But the mighty Wintapi wilderness that stretched away on all sides had not been changed, nor would it ever be. The towering summit of Stoney Lonesome still rose majestically in the haze-shrouded distance, and beyond that there was an almost endless succession of rolling, wooded mountains. Bear, deer, elk, lynx, game of all kinds, roamed in those fastnesses. The wilderness was also the haunt of numerous fur

animals which, in the old days, had provided a living
for Danny Pickett and his father.

Sean's interest had been aroused by the fact that
Danny Pickett was now swinging down a mountain
trail into the clearing. The big red dog was unable to
see Danny, but his scent was very plain. So were the
odors of the two Irish Setters with him. One was Big
Red, the other was Mike, Sean's blood brother.

Sean stood perfectly still, drinking in the luscious
scents and drooling a little at the mouth. Deep as the
heart within him was a longing to get out into the
mountains, to hunt and frolic as Mike and Red did.
So intense was this desire that Sean thought of little
else, and fretted because he was not permitted to go.

Born to hunt, and to be the companion of some
human being who liked to hunt, he had all the fine
instincts of a hunter. But it was Sean's misfortune
that he had also been born with an almost perfect
body. His head seemed molded by some master art-
ist. His spine and back and massive chest were
ideally formed, and his tail was a graceful brush that
drooped in precisely the right curve.

Sean was a show dog. Far too valuable to risk in the
wilderness, he was fast making his mark in the world
of dog shows. Though he was not yet two years old,
he had won easily in every class in which he had
been entered. He was certain to win his champion-
ship and equally certain, at the very least, to
give the national bench champions some stiff com-
petition.

He cared nothing about that, nothing about the
imposing array of ribbons and cups he had already

won for Mr. Haggin. He knew the show routine as well as the various handlers who took him into the ring. Almost Sean knew just what the judges wanted him to do next, and he never needed prompting to assume the correct stance. Still, from Sean's viewpoint, it was a very boring routine.

Sheilah, Sean's mother and now the mother of another litter of champions, ambled gracefully across the meadow to meet Danny, Red, and Mike. Sean whined anxiously. Woodsy smells, the enchanting scent of deep and seldom-visited places, clung to Danny and to the two dogs that had been out with him. Sean gave voice to a hopeful little bark, wanting to attract Danny's attention. At the same time, he knew the futility of such pleading. A hundred times he had tried it, with seldom a response.

Sean, like most dogs, was fond of Danny. But within his heart was a great empty space, and with a dog's inborn wisdom he knew that Danny would never fill that space. Danny's first love was still Big Red. His second was Mike, Sean's runt brother who never in his life would win first or even fourth place in any show. No true dog-lover's heart is big enough to enfold three dogs and to give all three an equal place. Irish Setters, who give all of themselves when they select a master, expect the master to give all in return. Nothing else will do.

With all of his full heart Sean longed for companionship such as Red and Mike had found. Anything less could not possibly be enough. Not just any human being, but one certain human, was what Sean desperately wanted.

His tail stopped wagging as Danny entered the handsome hunting lodge. Red and Mike, tired after their long walk in the mountains, stretched full length on the porch and slept. Sheilah, who was never chained or penned, joined them. A little on the timid side, the dainty Sheilah never went anywhere unless she was accompanied by either Danny or Ross Pickett. She preferred Ross because, from the very first, Sheilah had formed an attachment for him as strong as the love Red had for Danny. Independent Mike divided his affections between them.

Sean wandered to the far end of his run, sniffed halfheartedly at an ant that was crawling up the wall of his kennel, and swung hopefully to look toward the house. When Danny did not reappear, he lay down and dozed for a few minutes.

He awakened suddenly, fascinated by a scent that tickled his nostrils. But he did not at once raise his head or make any motion that might betray his presence. Thus he revealed more of his inherited wisdom. Anything that moved swiftly or jerkily was easy to discover, but a creature that lay still was very hard to see. Sean remained motionless, wanting to discover just what had interested him before he revealed his presence.

The scent continued to drift into his nose: a delicious, savory, soul-satisfying smell. Sometimes, when Danny or another hunter came in with grouse or quail, Sean had noticed a very similar odor. But always it had been at a distance. This was very near.

Sean rose slowly. His head was erect, his ears pricked, his eyes alight. For a moment he stood very still, drinking in heady draughts of the entrancing scent. Then he followed his nose toward it.

At the end of his run he was halted by the wire, and previous experience had taught him well that there was no way through or around that. Sean pushed his nose against the steel mesh and peered at the source of the scent.

Fifteen feet away a land terrapin—a small turtle —was chewing at a cluster of white mushrooms that had sprung up during the night. It stood there, armored shell protecting it, wrinkled legs pushed out as far as they would go, and horny head raised high to get at the best and choicest parts of the delicacy. The turtle, which knew very well that it need fear no enemy because it was protected by a coat of mail, had no thought save filling its belly. It did not have to think of anything except eating.

Sean was puzzled. The little terrapin bore not the slightest resemblance to a grouse, quail, pheasant, or other game bird. Yet the scent was much the same as a game bird's and it was certainly the odor that had attracted Sean. It was fascinating, the most intriguing scent that had ever blown into his nostrils.

Head pressed firmly against the wire, Sean studied the terrapin intently. The odor set his brain on fire; somehow he must get nearer the source of such a delicious thing. Yet there was no way. Sean whined and stepped back to paw at the wire.

He knew very well when Billy Dash, the kennel boy, emerged from a shed at the far end of the row of kennels. He still kept all his attention riveted on the terrapin and still wished that he knew some way to make it come to him. Try as he would, there just was no way. Sean turned his head to greet Billy Dash briefly and returned his attention to the turtle.

"Dog, you found somethin' you like, huh?"

The words were softly spoken, almost whispered, but they were remarkable because, when he was talking with another human being, Billy Dash seldom uttered three words in succession. He wouldn't talk even to Danny Pickett, his best friend. But when no one else was around he would talk by the hour to Sean.

"I reckon," Billy Dash said, "that I'll just take tem'tation right out of youah way. Then you won't have to fret you'self."

The lean hill youngster stooped, grasped the little terrapin by its hard shell, and picked it up. Legs searching futilely for a foothold and waving in all directions because they could not find any, the terrapin seemed a weird caricature of some huge and misshapen beetle as Billy Dash bore it away into the grassy field. He left his catch there and returned to Sean's kennel.

The watching dog saw a whip-thin youngster of about nineteen. A shock of brown hair, badly in need of cutting, tumbled down the side of Billy's head. His nose curved like a hawk's beak, his mouth was full and sensitive, and his eyes were as gentle and deep as a newborn fawn's. Yet, about him was a firm look that spoke of determination and courage.

Before coming to work for Danny, Billy Dash had lived where only the strong and quick survive. The youngest of ten children, he had been born back in the Wintapi wilderness. No roads led to his birthplace, only trails and footpaths, unknown to any save native mountaineers. Two clearings away lived Billy's Uncle Hat and his six male cousins, a quarrelsome, gun-happy tribe, not one of whom had ever done an honest day's work. Rather, they made periodic forays to hill farms and villages and stole whatever took their fancy. Fighting, with guns, knives, fists, or feet, was their principal recreation, and almost always they had a minor feud going with some other mountain clan. Occasionally the two Dash families conducted their own private feuds.

It was from such a place that Danny had brought Billy Dash to act as his kennel boy. Billy's present job was to clean the kennels and feed and exercise the dogs. But he would go beyond that. He was that rare person who has an inborn liking for and understanding of dogs. He seemed to know what they would have liked to tell him.

Turning occasionally toward the place where the terrapin had been, and where its odor still lingered, Sean watched with great pleasure as Billy Dash returned. Of all the humans he had ever met he liked Billy the best. There was something about the young hill man that struck a responsive chord deep within the big Irish Setter, but he had never bridged the gap completely. Between himself and Billy Dash there remained a barrier that Sean could sense but not understand. Billy grinned at him.

"Had you'self a time, Dog?"

Sean reared against the wire and bent a blissful head on Billy's chest. Gently, knowing exactly the right places, Billy tickled his ears with supple fingers. Sean sighed happily. This was what he wanted and liked. Gladly he would have given his whole heart to Billy Dash.

There remained the barrier, the wall that he was unable to break down. Sean could not possibly know that Billy Dash himself had built that wall, and for a good reason.

To Billy Dash this job was a Heaven-sent opportunity. He had a good bed in a clean house, as much wholesome food as he could eat, work that he loved, and seventy-five dollars a month to call his own. Few Wintapi hill men ever achieved so much. But the world of show dogs was outside Billy's ken.

The dogs he had known all his life, some of whom had been magnificent hunters, were curs and hounds that the mountaineers had used to course game. Almost never did a hill man buy a dog. Usually there was a nursing litter that would, in time, replace those killed by some fierce beast. If a mountaineer did take a fancy to a dog that he did not already own, he bartered, fought for it, or, all else failing, stole it. Surrounded by show dogs, any one of which was worth almost as much as he earned in a year, was too much for Billy Dash. He loved the Irish Setters, and was proud of his job, but he had been very careful not to win the affections of any dog because Danny or Mr. Haggin might not like it.

Yet, as he petted Sean, the inborn love that all born dog men feel for a magnificent dog shone in his eyes and showed in his face. Often Billy had dreamed of such a dog, but until he had seen Sean he had never thought one really existed. Sean seemed to him a queer name for such an animal, so Billy addressed the big Setter in his own fashion.

"You, Dog. Youah all dog. Seems mighty funny to keep you in a piddlin' little cage, and just use you fo' gettin' blue ribbons and little cups when you could be a huntin' dog. Seems mighty funny. Still, I s'pose it's impo'tant, else Danny and Mistah Haggin wouldn't do it. But fo' the life of me I can't figgah it."

Abruptly the spell was broken. Billy Dash stepped back from the wire and retreated into the shell he had built around himself. He went to and unlatched the kennel gate.

"Come on, Dog. Time to run."

Aquiver with excitement and nervous tension, Sean met him. A chance to stretch his superb legs was what he waited for all day long. He bounded through the open gate, brushed past Billy Dash, and raced in a mad circle that took him halfway to the forest's border. Whirling, he came back. Almost without pause he raced in another wild circle. Passing the kennel boy again, he leaped up and licked his cheek with a wet, sloppy tongue.

After ten minutes, his first wild energy spent, he went over and thoroughly snuffled the mushroom patch where the terrapin had been eating. Sean raised his head, testing the various breezes. At a slow trot that increased as he traveled, he started into the meadow. The terrapin's scent was faint on the breeze, but as Sean came closer the scent strengthened. Sean began to cast in wide circles that shortened as the scent became stronger. He found the terrapin where Billy Dash had put it down.

Experimentally Sean poked at it with an exploring paw. As though it worked on well-oiled joints, the terrapin's head glided beneath its hard shell. It drew in its legs and lay quietly. Sean scraped at the little turtle with his paw, turned it over on its back, and sniffed hard.

Billy Dash came softly up behind him.

"Not what you want, is it, Dog? No suh. Little old te'pin, that's not what you want at all. Shuah would like to get you out in the back lands with me, aftah real game."

Head bent, ears tumbling forward, Sean regarded the terrapin. Again he poked it with his paw, and turned it over. Then came a hail from the kennels.

"Billy."

"Yes suh."

With one last, lingering look at the terrapin, Sean fell in beside him as Billy Dash started back toward the kennels. He changed his smooth walk to an eager trot and raced ahead to greet Danny Pickett with wagging tail and questing nose. Big Red, a little jealous, stiffly sniffed noses with his handsome son. Absently Danny let his dangling hand stray over both dogs.

"How's it going, Billy?" he asked.

"Good."

"Do you need anything for the kennels?"

"No suh."

"Are all the dogs all right?"

"Yes suh."

"Things all right with you?"

"Yes suh."

Danny laughed. He was a hill man himself, and understood other hill men. "You're the talkative cuss, Billy!"

"Yes suh."

Danny handed Billy Dash a white envelope.

"Your two weeks' pay, Billy. By the way, Mr. Haggin and Mr. Jordan have decided to breed Sean with Jordan's Irisher, Penelope of Killarney. You're to take Sean over to Jordan's place next week."

Billy's eyes glowed. He had seen Penny, a champion in her own right and, next to Sean, Billy's idea of the most beautiful dog in the world.

"Yes suh," he said. "I'll have Sean ready."

Danny walked off with Big Red and Billy Dash let Sean continue his exercise. After an hour he pushed the reluctant dog back into his kennel run, latched the gate, and turned to other kennel chores. Ears flattened, begging with his eyes for Billy to come back, Sean watched him go. Then he lay down in his favorite spot beneath a maple tree.

Twilight lowered, and night folded softly over the Wintapi. Sean stretched, wandered into his kennel, and lay down to sleep. A moment later, he rose again. Four walls were confining, and usually gave him a sense of uneasiness. Most nights, even in very cold weather, he preferred to sleep in the wire run. Finding a soft spot on the clean earth, he curled up with his head resting on his flank.

Only a few stars glittered wanly in the sky when Sean arose again. He got up happily, eyes bright and tail wagging. Billy Dash was coming toward his kennel. Sean padded to the end of his run and reared against the wire. A moment later, a dim figure in the night, Billy Dash loomed over him.

"I come to say good night, Dog," he murmured. "Can't leave you heah the whole night long thinkin' that I fo'got all about you. You know I wouldn't do that."

Billy's fingers came through the wire to scratch Sean's ears, and Sean sighed blissfully. The young kennel man talked soothingly.

Suddenly Sean raised his head and stiffened. The bristles on his neck stood straight up, his tail was stiff behind him. Sean growled low in his throat. He continued to strain with questing nostrils into the eddying breeze and he growled again.

The breezes had brought to him a new scent, an odor laden with danger.

2. Uncle Hat

Sean held rigid, perfectly motionless, while he continued to test the winds. Warned by his almost inaudible growls that something was coming, Billy Dash turned and stood tensely against the wire run. Billy was a woodsman born. Sounds, scents, and noises that would have meant nothing to the average city man had their own meaning for him. But Billy lacked the extra-sharp senses of a dog, so he did not know that a man was coming.

Sean did know, and he was afraid of the scent that wafted to his nostrils. Just as Red and Mike knew by the scent of the various creatures they ran across whether or not such creatures intended to run away from them or to stay and fight, Sean knew that this man had hostile intentions.

The dimly lighted night revealed nothing except the misshapen outlines that buildings and trees usually display in darkness. Beyond these there were just scents and very faint sounds by which the oncoming man could be followed to advantage, and only Sean was able to interpret both scent and sound. He knew that the man had come out of the forest, in which he had been hiding, and started across the meadow. Sean followed him with his nose and ears.

The big dog turned his head for one more look at

Billy Dash. Since puppyhood Sean's every want and need had been taken care of by some human being. His own native initiative and resourcefulness had not been developed to that keen point which Mike and Big Red had achieved. Now, naturally, he looked to the nearest man he trusted to solve any problems that might arise here.

Out in the meadow a light thump sounded. Billy Dash whirled to face it.

"Howdy, Billy."

Sean heard Billy Dash's startled, "Uncle Hat!"

"Uncle Hat!" the other mocked him. "Uncle Hat! A body would think a boy'd be glad to see his own uncle, his own blood uncle, what he hadn't bothered to see in I dunno how many weeks. Ain't you glad to see me, Billy?"

Billy Dash said savagely, "No!"

"Gettin' uppity, eh?" Uncle Hat asked. "Never thought 'twould do you any good to hang 'round with rich folks thisaway. You get too uppity for yo'r own good, that's what you do."

As he approached in the very dim light, Uncle Hat showed himself to be a short man, lacking six inches of Billy's six feet. A battered felt hat sat well forward on his head, and uncut black hair straggled from beneath it. His eyes were pale, set close together. A bulbous nose protruded above a luxuriant growth of unkempt beard that concealed his mouth. He wore an old tattered suit coat, torn trousers, cut off at the knee, and heavy leather boots.

Uncle Hat still had a distinct air of authority. The huge .45 caliber revolver which, cocked and ready, he bore in his right hand, loaned that to him. The

gun's ugly muzzle was trained squarely on Billy
Dash.

There was a moment's silence, then Uncle Hat's
teeth gleamed faintly in the bushy beard. " 'No,' he
says! He ain't glad to see me! What you aim to do
about it, Billy?"

Billy Dash glanced downward, toward the revolver's ready muzzle.

"Nothin'."

"I see you ain't entirely took leave of your senses,"
Uncle Hat reflected. "But we might's well stop this
gibble-gabblin'. I want some money."

"Got no money."

"Oh, yes you have. Yes you have, Billy. I was up on
the slope, right behind a big oak tree, when I see
Danny Pickett give you some. Hand it over."

Without a word, Billy Dash took the unopened
envelope from his pocket and passed it over to Uncle
Hat.

Sean crouched low in his cage, still uncertain as to
the course he should adopt but not liking the sound
of the voices. He did not understand this. But he
knew that Billy Dash was in danger and, should a
fight come, he wanted to be in it on Billy's side. He
growled again, warningly.

Uncle Hat laughed.

"One of Haggin's fancy mutts, eh? Bet he couldn't
chomp his teeth through a platter of hot cornmeal
mush, and he's growlin' at me! Now let me see about
this."

The revolver in his right hand never wavering, he
used his left to tear the envelope open. Probing fin-

gers slipped inside. There was another moment of silence, then Uncle Hat's voice became ugly.

"Whar's the rest of it?"

"There's no mo'."

"Whar's the rest of it?"

"That's all."

"Billy, for the last time I'm askin'. No Dash ever worked like you have to for this much money. I want the rest and I want it now!"

"That's all! Now git!"

"I'll blast yo'r guts to the top of Stoney Lonesome! I'll—!"

A great roar of rage escaped Sean's chest. From up the line of kennels another dog echoed it, and a moment later all the dogs were in full-throated chorus. Sean leaped toward the top of his wire run, made a valiant effort to hook it with his front paws and scramble over, and fell back. He tried again, no longer in doubt as to what he should do and how he should do it. In the fight, on Billy's side, he must be. Never in his life had he bitten or even threatened a man, but he wanted to hurt this one. So intent was he on getting over the fence that he was heedless of everything else.

He did not see Billy, agile as a mink, duck low and come in fighting. Billy's steel-hard left hand shot out. His fingers closed around Uncle Hat's right wrist, and the gun was forced up. Supple as an eel, Billy twisted to one side, curled the fingers of his right hand around Uncle Hat's throat, and used his right elbow to block the blows of Uncle Hat's left fist.

The big revolver was the prize both wanted, and

their hands were locked on tilted arms as they strove
for it. Uncle Hat fought with all his strength to bring
the gun around to bear on Billy Dash. Cocked, the
revolver needed only the pressure of a finger to go
off.

There was a roar, a tongue of flame flashed from
the revolver's muzzle into the black night, and a
shadow flitted through the darkness. Uncle Hat lay
where he had fallen. Billy Dash was nowhere in
evidence.

And Sean was the only witness.

Danny Pickett was half asleep in the lodge. Lost in
the hazy world that is neither complete sleep nor full
wakefulness, he was with some amusement thinking
of how times had changed.

In the old days he and Ross had slept in one room,
while the loft of their cabin was reserved for the
hunters they guided or the fishermen they took to
various streams and ponds. They had cooked over a
wood stove, which had also heated the cabin, and
carried all their water from a spring. At night, the
cabin was lighted with kerosene lamps.

Now all that was changed. The lodge had accom-
modations for twelve guests, in addition to private
bedrooms for Ross, Danny, and Billy Dash. A gaso-
line-powered generator produced ample current to
provide all the electricity they could use. Bottled
gas, replenished at frequent intervals, fueled a modern gas range. The spring had been walled in, piped
into the house, and part of it ran through an automatic
hot-water heater. A bathroom boasted both a shower
stall and a tub. There was a gleaming refrigerator and

a deep-freeze unit in which food could be stored for long periods of time. In winter the lodge was heated by a central oil furnace. Even the road down to Mr. Haggin's had been graded and widened so cars could travel it at will.

Danny grinned faintly. There was something to be said for all the gadgets modern man had created—provided that he didn't go soft from using them. And there was little danger of it in these parts. The Wintapi slopes were just as steep as they'd ever been and the creeks were as swift. Anyone who prowled around them for several hours a day was certain to stay in first-class physical condition.

Red raised his head and growled softly. Danny roused from the slumber into which he was fast drifting.

"You, Red," he scolded. "Why don't you shut up?"

The big dog rose and padded across the floor to the screened bedroom window. He reared on the sill and pressed his nose against the screen so he could test the outside air. Again he growled softly.

"Listen," Danny said. "You can't sleep, so nobody else should either, huh? For pete's sake go back to bed and stop raising a racket!"

A second later Sean's throaty battle roar exploded in the night. The other kenneled dogs took up the challenge, turning what had been peace into bedlam.

Danny hit the floor with both feet, shucking off his pajamas as he did so and reaching for his clothes. Almost with the same motion he flicked the light switch on. Just as he did, he heard the blast of Uncle Hat's big .45.

In feverish haste Danny pulled a shirt over his head, zipped it shut without bothering to tuck it inside his trousers, and slipped his bare feet into moccasins. He snatched a double-barreled shotgun from a rack, loaded both barrels with buckshot, and jerked the door open.

Red stayed close beside him, bristled and ready. He knew what Danny did not, that Uncle Hat had paid the kennels a visit. And, like Sean, Red knew by the trespasser's scent that Uncle Hat's intentions were not good. But Red and Danny had been in trouble many times, and the big dog's experience told him they could meet every possible emergency.

The hall lighted suddenly as Danny flipped the switch. With Sheilah padding uneasily behind him, Ross burst out of his bedroom just as Danny started down the hall. Ross carried his favorite weapon, a 30-30 rifle. Father and son, having worked together for so long that there was no need for exchanging comments, looked at each other questioningly. Side by side, Red trotting ahead of them and Sheilah pacing behind, they ran into the kitchen. Danny threw the switch that controlled the kennel flood-lights, and they dashed onto the porch.

Flooded by brilliant white light, the kennels were revealed in every detail. Excited dogs, their tension heightened by the lights, leaped against their wire runs and fell back. Their barking made the night alive with noise.

Danny and Ross raced across the grass. Both had seen the crumpled figure lying in front of Sean's run. Danny kept his shotgun ready and his eyes on Red. Who had shot one man here tonight might not be at all unwilling to shoot two. They reached the fallen man and Ross bent over him.

"Hat Dash!"

Danny's voice expressed his relief. "I was afraid it might be Billy."

The two looked meaningly at each other. If Billy Dash was still at the kennels, he would be with them now. Again there was no need for speculation. What had happened here was all too evident.

"Where Hat Dash goes, trouble goes," Ross said tensely.

"He sure brought it here. Billy didn't go into the mountains to find him."

"Boy, I'm not sayin' you're wrong. But why should Hat come here to raise a fuss?"

"I paid Billy today."

"I see." For a moment Ross stared soberly into the night, then he turned to the man on the ground. "Well, we can't leave him here."

Ross knelt beside Hat Dash and slipped a hand beneath his coat. For a moment he held still, as though uncertain of what he had found. He looked up at Danny.

"He's still alive," he said, "but not too much alive. We'd best not try to move him. Get me some blankets, Danny. Then phone Mistah Haggin."

When Danny returned with the blankets, Ross had cut away the wounded man's coat and shirt and had loosened his belt. Danny glanced soberly at Hat's wound, just below his ribs. It was a very small hole, with only a few drops of blood, but Danny knew what he would find should he look at the place where the bullet had come out. If Hat Dash lived to tell of this he was going to be the luckiest man in the Wintapi.

Silently Ross held up a white envelope.

"Billy's pay. Found it in Hat's pocket."

"How about the gun?"

"It's not here. Billy must of took it. Where he's goin' he'll need that more than money. You go ahead and phone."

Danny went back into the lodge, picked up the phone, and gave the two short rings that called Mr. Haggin's house. He waited a moment, and then Mr. Haggin himself answered the phone.

"Hello?"

"Hello. This is Danny, Mr. Haggin, Danny Pickett. There's been trouble, a shooting."

"Who was shot?"

"Hat Dash. Look, I'll tell you all about it when you get here. We need a doctor and an ambulance, bad."

There was a short pause. Then Mr. Haggin said, "It seems to me that we need the police, too."

Danny said reluctantly, "Maybe we do."

"All right. I'll be there as soon as possible."

Danny hung up and went back out to where Ross knelt beside the still figure under the blankets. Danny shifted his feet uneasily. The night was not a particularly cold one, but it seemed to him that it was. He glanced at Ross, who shook his head, and they sat down to watch the road leading from the Haggin estate.

Finally, the lights of two cars pierced the blackness. A sleek ambulance drew up in front of the lodge, and a black and white State Police car pulled in behind it.

Danny, Ross, and Mr. Haggin stood aside while the efficient young doctor worked over Hat Dash. At last the doctor and the ambulance driver lifted Hat onto a stretcher and put him in the ambulance. Mr. Haggin broke the silence.

"What are his chances, doctor?"

"One in a hundred."

"Bad, eh?"

"Very bad. I think the lung is punctured. We'll have to operate—if he lives that long."

The ambulance glided smoothly down the road, and it seemed to Danny that he could breathe again. Life had been in the presence of Death, but now Death was gone, under the care of the doctor in the ambulance, and Life could resume its normal course. One of the efficient men in the gray uniform of the State Police turned to Danny.

"Who was the wounded man?" he asked.

"Hatley Dash."

"Do you know who shot him?"

Danny fumbled, almost blurted out Billy's name, then said, "No, I don't."

The gray-clad trooper looked at him coldly, and Danny felt his face flame. Mr. Haggin broke the silence.

"Corporal Graves and Constable Malone, meet Danny and Ross Pickett. I'm sure they're not responsible."

Corporal Graves softened, and asked, "Who do you *think* shot him?"

Danny said unwillingly, "I think it must have been his nephew, Billy Dash."

"Who is he?"

"Our kennel boy," Danny said. "Before he came to work for us, he lived up on Cummerly Knob."

"Was there bad blood between nephew and uncle?"

"I don't think so."

Mr. Haggin broke in. "Where is Billy, anyway?"

"He's gone."

"The crazy kid," Mr. Haggin murmured. "He might better stay and face it."

Corporal Graves took over again. "Gone, eh? Suppose you tell us what you know about this."

"Dad and I were in bed when Red—that's this dog right here—growled. I figured it was some animal, then Sean, another of our dogs, let out a bellow. The rest of the dogs joined in, and I heard a revolver shot. When we ran out, Hat was on the ground in front of Sean's run."

"That's all you know?"

"That's all."

"All right, Danny. Now suppose you tell us what you think happened."

"I paid Billy today. Hat must have somehow known that I did. He came down for Billy's pay, and threatened him with a gun. After Billy handed the money over they probably scuffled for the gun and Hat was shot. Billy must have been scared and ran away."

"That's your opinion?"

"That's it."

"Was Billy the sort to pick a fight?"

"No!"

"How about Hat?"

Danny said drily, "Hat wasn't exactly a pacifist. You know these mountaineers."

"Well, we'll have to pick Billy up. Can you take us to his house?"

"Sure. But—"

"But what?"

"Nothing," Danny said.

The State Police were handling this. Plainly they expected Billy Dash to run for home. They might find him there, and then again they might not. In Danny's opinion, home was the last place in the world that Billy Dash would head for.

Sean was more than a little worried, and thoroughly mystified by the strange doings of the humans. Danny and the State Police, their natty uniforms wrinkled and dirty and a stubble of beard shading their faces, had come down out of the mountains alone. The uniformed men had waited around for a whole day, and seemed more than a little angry. Then they had left.

Every afternoon, always at the hour Billy Dash had taken him out for exercise, Sean waited hopefully at the kennel gate. Billy did not come; even his well-remembered scent was fading. Danny had not yet been able to get another kennel boy and both Danny and Ross were far too busy to give all the dogs as much attention as they should have had. Only Sheilah, Red and Mike, dogs that normally ran free all the time anyway, had been outside the kennels.

It was very boring. Sean had hunted ants until he was weary of it, snapped at flies until he was tired of that too, and was even bored with stalking the mouse. Though by all normal standards his cage was big enough, there was really not enough room for Sean to stretch his legs as he wanted to stretch them. There had been no mad dashes through the meadow, none of the mile-long races that he loved.

Then, one morning, a small pickup truck came up from the Haggin estate. The truck's body was fitted with stakes over which a tarpaulin stretched tightly. Sean knew the truck and its purpose as well as Red knew what would follow when Danny started cleaning his shotgun. But he did not like riding in the truck, and crawled way back in his kennel. It did no good, because Danny called him out. Sean flattened his ears in sad resignation.

Released from his cage, he trotted slowly beside Danny, waited until the truck's gate was lowered, and jumped up. Without being bidden, he entered the slatted dog crate inside the truck and lay down. The crate's door was latched and the tail gate raised back into place. Sean heard Danny give last-minute instructions to the driver.

"Sorry I have to send you alone, Joe. I'd hoped to have Billy go along too. But—" Danny shrugged eloquently.

"Any news of Billy?" the truck driver asked.

"Not a sign."

"How about Hat?"

"He's alive, and that says about everything."

"Poor Billy," the truck driver commented. "Too bad he got himself into a scrape like that. Somebody else should have shot Hat—and twenty years ago."

"Yeah," Danny agreed. "Now you deliver Sean

personally to Tom Jordan, on the Pococimo Road. You know where it is, don't you?"

"Sure thing, Danny. But I wish the station wagon hadn't gone on the fritz. This old crate ought to be junked."

"Well, take it easy. We won't expect you back until late tonight."

Sean adjusted himself to the jolting motion as the truck bounced down the road, rolled past the Haggin estate, and entered a highway. The driver picked up speed, and for the first twenty miles the truck ran smoothly. Then there was a slight squealing, a loud noise, and the truck, on three good tires, lurched to a halt on the road's shoulder.

Sean looked on, mildly interested and not at all alarmed as the driver got out, looked disgustedly at the blown tire, and began to replace it with the good spare. Presently they were rolling again, out of the wilderness and past fat farms. Again the truck came to a sputtering halt. Once more the driver alighted.

"Hound," he said to Sean, "you're a jinx."

The driver raised the hood and began to tinker with the engine, but it was a full hour before they started again. Meantime Sean relaxed in his cage. He didn't know where they were going and he didn't much care, but as long as the truck wasn't jouncing him about he was content to lie still and sniff the strange scents that drifted into his crate.

They passed through the farming country back into forested hills. Sean's interest heightened. These woodsy smells were much more to his liking. Then, a second time within a few hours, there was the smacking jolt of a blown tire and the truck limped to the

road's shoulder. The driver stared at the tire help-
lessly, then looked balefully at Sean.

"Now we *are* in a mess! Ten miles to the nearest
town and no spare! Who'd think you could cause so
much trouble in only one day?"

He jacked the truck up, removed the blown tire,
and sat down on a rear fender. But almost three-
quarters of an hour elapsed before another car came
along. The driver hailed it down.

"Take this into Arnold's Garage at Clover, will
you? Ask him to bring a new one and this spare back
as soon as he can. Tell him I have to stay here and
watch over one of Dick Haggin's million-dollar
mutts. He should hustle. Thanks a lot."

The sun was beginning to lower when the trouble
car came with the necessary tires. The driver and the
mechanic put one on the truck and the other on the
spare wheel. When the mechanic had left, the driver,
again ready to go, called back to Sean.

"Hope you won't mind a few jolts, dog. But if I'm
going to get back at all tonight I have to step on it, and
I know a couple of short cuts. Here we go."

He swerved from the macadam onto a dirt road,
and began to climb. Sean lay still, entirely delighted.
This was the sort of country he liked. Both sides of
the road were heavily forested, and enchanting
odors came from the woods. Sean smelled rabbits,
grouse, deer, and once a panther that had crossed the
road no more than a minute or two ahead of the truck.

There was a sudden thunderous clatter that
seemed to be directly beneath him, and Sean was
startled. But the driver, muttering under his breath,

merely increased his speed. The truck's muffler had blown and little else could be heard.

The truck bounced on a boulder, careened to another one, and bumped over a whole nest of them. Sean looked with interest at the tail gate. Both latches had come unhitched, and the gate was flapping behind the truck. But they did not slacken speed.

Sean braced his feet and sat up. He seemed to be sliding, and that made him nervous. He looked down, past the side of the road, into a deep ravine that was floored with a tangle of rhododendron and laurel. The truck hit another rough spot. The dog crate jounced high, slid sideways, spilled out the back end, struck the road, and bounded into the ravine.

All unaware, the driver roared on.

3. Wanderers

When the big .45 went off, and Uncle Hat dropped to the ground, Billy Dash leaned for a second against Sean's kennel run to regain his spent breath. Then he sprang into action.

He was the only gentle and even-tempered male among the entire clan of Dashes, and it had never been his wish to hurt anyone or anything. At the same time, Billy had learned long before he was in his teens that in the wilderness mere survival sometimes carries a high price tag. When circumstances demand it, whoever or whatever doesn't fight doesn't live either. This fight had been thrust upon him, and if he had not hurt Uncle Hat he would have been hurt himself. It was as simple as that, and the fact that the revolver had gone off accidentally made no difference.

He felt great regret, but it was not sorrow for Uncle Hat, who had deliberately brought trouble. Billy knew that he himself would be lying there if Uncle Hat was not. He felt only a soul-searing disappointment because, all in the space of a few fleeting second he had seen his brightest dreams destroyed.

His relatives had jeered and ridiculed him when he went to work for Danny, but he had gone just the same. For the first time in his life he had found some of the things that he had always wanted, and there was a promise of more. Some day, like Danny, he might own one of those wonderful dogs. Maybe even a dog like Sean. Meanwhile he had wanted to continue working for Danny. Though he was not interested in dog shows, he knew very well that he could train the Irish Setters to hunt, as Danny had done with Big Red. That was what he had hoped to do.

However, there was no chance of that now. Things were as they were, and all the hard work and wishing in the world could not make them otherwise. Problems were best faced squarely and realistically.

He stooped, picked up the revolver, unbuckled the holster and beltful of cartridges that Uncle Hat wore, and strapped it around his own waist. He thrust the revolver into its sheath. Hastily he tapped Uncle Hat's pockets. Finding another box, half filled with cartridges, he slipped it into his shirt pocket and faded into the darkness.

Never once did it occur to him that he should stay and try to fight things through. He knew only that he had shot a man, and such actions always brought the law. No Dash, involved with the law or with an officer of the law, had ever come out ahead. They always lost, so the best thing was not to be caught.

Billy did not run; he was too woods-wise to flee blindly or to be panicked into anything foolish. He knew perfectly well that the pitch-black night shielded him. Give him twenty yards start on such a night and a thousand pursuers couldn't catch him. Only with the coming of daylight would he be in any danger.

He trotted across the meadow and into the forest.

There he halted. Standing beside the gray trunk of a huge beech tree, he saw the lights come on in the lodge. A second later the kennels were floodlighted. If Uncle Hat weren't already dead, he would be looked after.

Billy leaned numbly against the tree, and again a bitter disappointment rose within him. Then he turned away from the life he would have loved and did not look back again.

He climbed the side of the mountain, making no special effort to avoid noise. Nobody was coming after him tonight and if they did they couldn't catch him. But tomorrow he must at all costs avoid being seen. If an officer, or anyone else, should find him and demand his surrender, Billy was not sure that he could use a gun. He still had no wish to hurt anyone, and the best way to make certain he wouldn't have to fight again was to keep out of everyone's sight.

Reaching the top of the mountain, he rested. Though he hadn't climbed fast, he had walked steadily, and was winded. Also, he wanted to plan out the rest of his flight.

It was, of course, unthinkable to go home. That was partly a point of honor, for he did not want to run the risk of involving others of the clan. Also, Uncle Hat's quarrelsome sons were there, and Billy wanted no more trouble.

The mountain top was an almost solid bed of rock, with a thin layer of topsoil here and there. Green grass grew wherever there was such a place, as well as a few big beech trees and smaller scrub. Billy chose his way carefully, feeling a path with his feet and keeping on the rock as much as possible. He doubted if they'd set bloodhounds on him because there were none in the Wintapi as far as he knew. There were some very expert trackers, both dog and human, but Billy was not unduly worried by them because he was just as expert at hiding his trail. Also, many of the trackers were his friends. Even if they were hired or persuaded to track him down, there was some doubt that they would try very hard.

He walked on, his mind made up. Last winter, before he went to work for Danny, he had lived in a lonely cabin twenty miles from his home on Cummerly Knob. All winter he had lived there, running a trap line, avoiding his relatives, and snowshoeing into Centerville whenever he needed supplies. Billy wanted to be into and out of that cabin a full two hours before daylight.

It was about half-past two when he reached the cabin. He squatted on his haunches out there in the darkness, waiting to see whether or not the place was occupied. There was no smell of fresh wood smoke, and the path leading to the cabin was weedgrown. Going up the path, Billy halted ten feet from the door, stooped to pick up a stone, and threw it against the door. He heard it strike, and fall back. There was no challenge.

Billy opened the door, entered, and groped on the table. A tin can full of matches was where he had left it. He struck one, by its rising flare located a stub of candle, and lighted it. The candle looked the way he remembered it, its own melted wax holding it upright in a cracked dish.

Obviously the cabin had not been occupied since he left it. A thick pall of dust overlay everything, and the table was laced with delicate tracks where hungry deer mice had lately wandered across it. Billy looked at his storage shelf.

There were four tightly capped tins there, and scrawled across them in pencil was an index of their contents: coffee, sugar, salt, and flour. In addition there were a few cans of dried fruits and vegetables. None of it would tempt a plunderer.

Billy put the lighted candle on the floor, went to the cabin's end floor board, and pushed with his foot. The board tilted to reveal a concealed hiding place. This compartment beneath the floor had been his storage space, the place where he kept everything that he did not carry with him and did not dare take home. Anyone coming into the cabin, Billy hoped, would never suspect that it contained ánything except the few odds and ends that were visible on the shelves.

From his hiding place Billy withdrew a wrapped .22 repeating rifle, a carton of cartridges for it, a small can of cleaning solvent, a can of oil, a pair of moccasins, a shirt and coat, a hand axe, a pack sack, a dozen and a half steel traps, some fishing tackle, and an oilskin packet which, when opened, revealed fifteen one-dollar bills.

Billy looked speculatively at the money. He hadn't even thought to take his two weeks' wages back from Uncle Hat, and money could serve him well. Thankfully he tucked the fifteen dollars into an inside pocket and began to assemble the rest of his gear on the table.

Everything except the rifle and axe he stowed in the pack sack, and those he lashed to the side of his load. For a moment he deliberated. Others knew of the cabin. They knew it was his, and anyone coming to it within the next day or so would surely know that he had been there. That chance he would have to take. If he burned the cabin its glow could be seen in the darkness and he dared not tarry there after daylight.

Twenty steps from the cabin's door he plunged into a tangle of rhododendron which, even had it been viewed in daylight, would have seemed impenetrable. Billy entered unhesitatingly. Deer and elk abounded in this section of the Wintapi and the rhododendron thicket was a wide belt that divided two favorite grazing pastures. When they did not have to hide, animals were not partial to crashing their way through brush, and so the thicket was laced with trails. Billy knew all of them.

Dawn was just breaking with he emerged on a high, heavily forested peak. This was one of the wildest parts of the Wintapi; the nearest passable highway was miles away. Billy dropped his pack, overturned rocks, caught a few of the big black crickets that crawled beneath them, and rigged his fishing rod. A streamlet, hardly more than a trickle of water, curled down from the peak. But Billy's first cast produced an eight-inch trout. He caught another and then missed one. When he had six, he salted them sparingly, cooked them over a tiny fire, and ate. That done, he kicked his fire into the streamlet, concealed with pine needles the place where it had burned, and slept.

Sean opened his eyes and tried hard to stand up

because he thought he heard Billy Dash calling him. He arose on rubbery legs which, as soon as he braced them, melted down to nothingness and sent him sprawling across the slatted side of the wooden crate. The big Setter lapsed back into the unconsciousness out of which he had valiantly forced himself.

Totally unprepared for the crate's falling, Sean had made no effort whatever to do anything about it. Striking the road, he had been flung violently against the heavy floor boards, and had been only vaguely aware when the crate tumbled down into the rhododendrons. Instead of breaking, the tough, resilient stalks had bent to admit and then fold around the crate. Now it was hidden. No casual passerby, traveling up the road, could tell by looking that the crate had fallen off at this point. It would take the trained eye of a woodsman to detect it.

A second time Sean stirred, and then raised a sick head to look dazedly at the surrounding brush. A rhododendron, bending under the weight of the crated dog, had thrust a slim branch within the crate and the dangling, long leaves brushed Sean's ear. He shook his head to relieve the tickling, and when he did, the motion brought extreme dizziness. The spell passed and he felt better.

He panted heavily, his jaws wide and tongue dangling its full length. A raging thirst consumed him. Worst of all, he was completely bewildered.

He remembered being on the truck, with a man who would attend his every want close at hand, and now he was here. Without knowing why, Sean realized that this should not have happened. Many times he had ridden on the truck and in the station .

wagon. Always he had arrived safely, gone through whatever ritual he was supposed to perform, and returned safely to Danny's clearing. Feeling helpless and terribly alone, Sean whimpered softly.

Then his native intelligence and the resourcefulness bequeathed to him by Big Red asserted itself. He was all alone and abandoned, but it was not in him to give way to hopelessness. His nose told him that there was no man around. He himself must do something about this and do it soon.

The crate lay on its side, tilted against the boulder that had finally halted its downward plunge. Sun filtered through the slats to dapple Sean's rich fur. He stood up, but when he did his back and shoulders touched the slats on the upper side. He held his aching head low to keep from bumping it again.

The door, he knew, was at one end. But he was still dazed and sick, so that not at once could he determine which end. Sean lowered a probing nose and pushed at what he thought was the door. When it did not open, he pushed harder.

Puzzled and exasperated, he accidentally rose up higher than he had intended to. In all his experience he had known just one way to get into and out of a crate—through the door. Yet, when he raised himself to his full height, his shoulders pushed against the upper slats and he felt them yield.

Sean stood a moment, not at once sure of the full significance of such a thing. But there was something about the yielding slats that gripped his attention. Again, very cautiously, he pushed his shoulders against the loose slats. Again they yielded.

The crates were made to hold the biggest,

strongest, and wildest dog. But they had not been
made to endure a fall from the back of a speeding
truck and a tumble down a boulder-studded slope.
The crate, in falling, had split one of the supports that
held the slats. The screws that clamped the slats
down had loosened. Sean pushed again, felt the slats
rise, and pawed frantically against their loose ends.
Roughly, heedless of the fact that he was further
hurting his already bruised head, he shoved it
through, pulled with his front feet and pushed with
his rear ones until he had scrambled over the side of
the crate to freedom.

Within itself it was a minor act, yet it showed the
Setter's inheritance. In spite of his sheltered life and
his almost complete dependence on human beings,
Sean had just proven that he had an all-important
talent which could be called upon when problems
confronted him. He had the ability to think for himself.

Now that he was free, some of his waning confidence returned. Gone was the sensation that he had
been wholly abandoned and was helpless because of
it. Since he was an animal, concerned only with the
present and never worried about the future, Sean
knew only that he was terribly thirsty.

He was also still weak and wobbly. Partly because
it was easier to travel downhill, and partly because
his good sense told him that he would be more likely
to find water in that direction, he started down
through the rhododendrons. Unskilled at this sort of
travel, he slowed his beginning run to a trot and then
to a walk. It was better to go slowly than to become
constantly entangled in the rhododendrons.

Coming to the bottom of the valley, and finding it dry, Sean continued to obey the instinct that told him he would find water sooner by traveling downhill than he would by climbing up. A mile and a half from where he had wriggled out of the crate he finally discovered the water that he had been looking for.

Two large boulders, their ancient sides covered with moss and lichens, stood side by side at the base of a steep little down-slope. Between them, a crystal-clear spring bubbled out of the valley's floor and formed a small pool. A few small trout, flitting shadows in the water, fled frantically at Sean's approach. The big dog stood a moment, licked his chops hungrily, and sprawled full length to lap up prodigious draughts of the ice-cold water.

He raised his head, and water dripped from both sides of his open mouth to tinkle musically back into the spring. A pert blue jay, half-hidden by the green leaves of a white oak, peered curiously at him. The jay voiced a couple of experimental squawks, hoping for sport. When Sean paid no attention to him, the jay ruffled his feathers angrily. He squawked again, louder. Still unable to draw Sean's attention, he flew indignantly away.

Wholly absorbed in his own problems, Sean had neither eyes nor ears for anything else. He stepped into the water, feeling a delicious thrill as it lapped around his legs and plastered his fur down. Sean lay down, so the icy water could flow over his back. Three times he clamped his jaws, and then stopped panting.

Sean was not a fragile human being, but a tough, hardy animal. Hurt, he would either die quickly or recover quickly. Only in exceptional cases, when everything is very favorable, can animals undergo a long period of convalescence.

The cold water restored Sean's sense of balance and banished his weakness. When he emerged from the pool his head throbbed faintly, but that was all.

Now he should begin to find a way out of his predicament. He shook his wet fur, paced restlessly back and forth, and again whimpered uneasily. A dismal loneliness recurred; he hadn't the least idea as to what to do next. Even Big Red, with all his woods wisdom, would have found it hard to discover an answer to this riddle.

Sometimes, when they were hunting and more often when they were just rambling, Red and Danny became separated. But almost never was Red taken anywhere in a car, and so he knew every inch of the Wintapi. Consequently, if for any reason he was unable to pick up Danny's trail, and follow him home, he knew the way himself. But Sean did not know the way home. Since leaving the Pickett clearing the truck had traveled about a hundred and sixty miles, and Sean had no idea where he was.

He made his forlorn way back to the crate and lay down beside it. Darkness descended, bringing with it all the alien scents and sounds that only deep night in the wilderness produces. A prowling lynx, come to hunt rabbits in the rhododendron thicket, smelled the dog and faded silently away on its oversized paws. At the same time Sean smelled the lynx. He knew from its scent that it was afraid of him, and running away.

Stabbing the night with its headlights, a car went up the lonely road. Sean raised his head, but not with any special hopefulness. He knew by its sound that the car was not the one from which he had fallen. It never occurred to him that anyone save the truck driver would come searching for him.

Sean could not know another and very important fact: the truck driver had made a mistake. Ten miles farther on, and seven miles from Tom Jordan's place on the Pococimo Road, the truck's wheels had thrown up a boulder that thumped heavily against the under-carriage. The driver remembered the incident and the place, and when it was discovered that Sean was missing he had decided that the sound he had heard must have been the crate falling. Though a frantic search for Sean had been organized, no searcher had yet come within eight miles of the place where the dog actually was.

Gray morning floated like a mist over the wilderness and still Sean waited near the wrecked crate. Briefly he left to get another drink of water, then in a flurry of panic returned to the crate, the one familiar thing he knew. But another spur was goading him now.

He had eaten nothing in almost thirty-six hours; Danny did not feed his dogs before starting them out on a long trip because, if they were fed, danger of trip-sickness increased. Had Sean arrived at Tom Jordan's when he was supposed to, he would have eaten well. But he hadn't, and now he was famished.

The morning was half gone when he left the crate for the last time. He walked purposefully, unswervingly, with no intention of coming back. If anyone was coming to get him, they would have done so before this.

The big Setter lacked the faintest idea of where he was going. He only knew that somehow he must find and give himself over to a human being. He started directly into the wilderness.

He did not travel in a circle, as a lost man might have done. Though he had been sheltered and protected all his life, by every natural instinct he was still closer to elemental things than the keenest man ever can be. Though they were dormant in Sean, all the senses of his wild ancestors were still with him, and he instinctively traveled as a wild dog would have traveled.

A buck deer, browsing among some oaks, snorted and stamped his hoof as Sean approached, then whirled and fled with his upraised white tail marking his line of flight. Sean's tongue lolled, and an Irish Setter grin showed on his face. In spite of gnawing hunger, he was thoroughly enjoying this, his first real run in the woods.

Suddenly Sean halted, nose quivering and mouth drooling as a sudden delicious odor wafted to his nostrils. Forty feet ahead a mother grouse and her brood of half-grown, bob-tailed young were dusting themselves in an old ant hill. Sean stood still, body tense and one fore paw curled up from the ground. Involuntarily, he had snapped into a perfect point. But Sean knew nothing about holding a point. After a few seconds he broke and charged the brood.

The grouse rose on drumming wings and sped away. Eagerly, nostrils working and tail waving,

Sean snuffled thoroughly the places where they had been. Only after three-quarters of an hour did he pace on.

He was among beech trees now, gray-trunked giants much like the beeches of the Wintapi. Sean swerved, attracted by a colorful something high on the trunk of one of the beeches. It was a cluster of beefsteak mushrooms, still tender and so fresh that, in the shady grove, dewdrops still clung to them.

Sean reared against the trunk, sniffed at the mushrooms, and dropped back to study them further. His head was bent to one side, his ears cocked questioningly. Again he reared, took a bit of mushroom in his mouth, tasted it with his tongue, and swallowed it. The taste was not at all unpleasant, so Sean took a large mouthful. He ate all the mushrooms he could reach and looked longingly at those he could not.

They were by no means a satisfying meal, but they blunted the keenest edges of his appetite. Sean trotted on. He stopped to drink from another sparkling little trout stream, and then, just before the twilight shadows began to lower, he raised a happy head.

From somewhere in the distance, far-off and faint but unmistakable, came the odor of man. Sean increased his trot to a delighted gallop. For endless hours he had been lost and desperately lonely. Now, at last, he would find the companionship he craved. He came to a clearing in the forest, and halted.

About five acres in all, the clearing was one of three that were separated by thin belts of trees. In the center was an unpainted cabin, much like the one Danny and Ross had lived in before their lodge was built. Near the cabin was a ramshackle barn that was slowly falling apart under the combined and endless impact of sun, wind, rain, and snow. Grouped in a corral adjoining the barn were thirty-five sheep, their wool matted with burrs and leaves. There were also a black and white cow and a brown horse.

Sean hesitated because it was his nature to hesitate. No Irish Setter is vicious, and all of them like humans, but they react to people differently. Some fling themselves gaily upon whoever comes, some are reticent and must be sure of a welcome before they will make friends with strangers. Sean was of the latter temperament.

For a moment he stood within the forest's border, then took a step into the clearing. He saw a man dressed in faded blue jeans and a checkered shirt come out of the cabin and stand on the porch. Sean flattened his ears and wagged his tail to show that he had only the most amiable of intentions. The man went back into the cabin, reappeared almost immediately, and walked slowly in Sean's direction.

The dog could not know that this was the cabin and clearing of Jake Busher, or that Jake had good reason to fear and hate most things that came out of the forest into his clearing. Working hard to build up a flock of sheep, one of the few money crops that would flourish on his thin acres, Jake had already seen almost half his flock pulled down and killed by four-footed raiders. Now he saw only another pirate, coming to claim more tribute.

Sean advanced another step, his ears still flattened and the tip of his tail wagging appeasingly. There was a sudden crashing back in the forest as a lightning-riven limb fell from its parent tree. Startled, Sean turned to look.

The fact that he was looking away from the man rather than toward him probably saved Sean's sight. Jake Busher's shotgun roared, and like hot, angry bees, lead pellets snicked into Sean's neck and shoulder. He leaped convulsively, whirled, and streaked back into the shelter of the forest. The shotgun blasted again.

The second shot did little harm. Sean was so far away that no pellet did more than penetrate his thick fur and sting a little.

4. Slasher

Even when he was hidden by the friendly forest, Sean did not stop running. This was a new and terrible experience. Of the thousands of people he had seen, at dog shows and at the Haggin estate, almost all had stopped to admire him. Never before in his whole life had any human being hurt him or tried to hurt him.

His neck and left shoulder seemed on fire where the leaden pellets had buried themselves. He lifted his left front paw from the ground and raced along on three legs. This eased the pain, but did not stop it. However, Sean was not the kind of dog to let his hurts panic him or make him race away in wild hysteria.

His first and instantaneous reaction had been to put a safe distance between himself and Jake Busher. As soon as he had done so he circled to bring himself in a position where he could test the winds. This was an instinctive act; a knowledge of how to do such things was born in Sean. No animal could successfully fight an enemy without knowing where that enemy was, what he was doing, and, if possible, what he planned to do next.

Sean slowed to a limping walk, and crept into a patch of thick laurel. A brown weasel, a foot of whip-thin muscle and fury, snarled silently at him and glided like a snake beneath a moss-grown log. Sean paid no attention as he passed. Before he did anything else, he must find out what had happened to Jake Busher and whether or not Jake was pursuing him.

The intertwined leaves of the laurel formed an almost sun-proof canopy above him, but Sean could thread a hidden way among the crooked stalks. He emerged from the laurel onto an aspen-covered little rise and ran across that as fast as three legs could take him. The aspens were open and he must not be seen. He ran down the other side of the rise and into another laurel patch.

Gradually he circled on a course that took him almost directly back toward Jake Busher's clearing. He cut around so that he was running almost parallel to his former trail, then slowed to a walk. Every few minutes he halted and did not move until the shifting breezes brought him the exact story of what lay ahead. Presently he found the scent of the clearing in his nostrils.

This was like the game he had played with the mouse, only now Sean's life was at stake if he lost. The dog could do nothing except depend on his own wits and inborn knowledge. These told him that a moving thing was easy to see but a motionless object, even if it could be seen, was always hard to identify. Sean halted in a thick copse of saplings and lay perfectly still. He was within one hundred yards of the trail he had made when he fled from Jake Busher, and less than fifty yards from the edge of the clearing.

Sean read the story with his nose. Jake Busher had

followed him a ways; the scent of Jake's tracks was mingled with the odor of Sean's trail. But Jake had gone back to the cabin and was there now. His scent told Sean that much—and no more.

The big Setter lay still for a long while. The fact that Jake was in his cabin did not necessarily mean that he would stay there.

Night had fallen when Sean left the vicinity of the clearing to make his way back into the forest. Highly intelligent, quick to respond to influences about him, he had learned a very harsh lesson the hard way. From now on he must be wary not only of Jake Busher, but of all men whom he did not know. Never again must he trust himself within reach of a stranger. At the same time he retained a great curiosity about Jake Busher and the clearing, and had a compelling desire to know more of them. But right now there were other things to do.

His neck and shoulder throbbed painfully, felt hot, and the wounds had made him feverish. However, now that he had satisfied himself about his enemy's whereabouts, it was time to go. Sean was too close to the clearing, and entirely aware of the fact that Jake Busher might find him again. What he wanted was some safe retreat where he could be alone.

No longer hungry, because of his pain, he was very thirsty. When he came to a cold little stream he stopped to drink, then lay down in a shallow pool. The water's icy touch was soothing, and his injuries did not hurt quite so fiercely as he lay in the pool. But because he was still too near Jake Busher's cabin, he got up and went on.

For hours he traveled, setting a straight course that

carried him away from man and into the haunts of wild animals. The night was two-thirds gone when he finally discovered just what he had been looking for.

He had come to another of the little streams that trickled down every main valley and every tributary gully, and turned upstream. Where the stream entered the valley, he found himself in a thicket of high bush huckleberries. Sean splashed through puddles as he made his way among them to the very center of the thicket, where he discovered a few aspen trees and a pool of clear water. Huckleberries grew profusely among the aspens, and around the pool.

When Sean found the pool, the water was at the normal summer level. But bordering it on all sides was a bed of rich mud and silt created by spring floods of melting snow. It was in this mud that the huckleberries found a rooting.

Sean sighed gratefully. He lay down in the cold mud and pressed his left side firmly into it. That did not cover his neck wounds, so with a struggle he sat up and used his right front paw to scrape a hole. When he lay down in that, the wet mud oozed over his back, covering him almost completely. Only his head protruded from the hole.

The sun rose, and Sean remained absolutely motionless in his mud bath. Over his head rose a shielding growth of huckleberries. His body was completely submerged in cold mud, which cooled the air for a few inches above it, so that no flies or mosquitoes bothered him. His eyes were half-closed and he breathed hard. His nose was very hot.

After a while he raised his head to lap thirstily from

a little water-filled depression, then lay down again. He did not want to move because his every instinct told him that it was better not to.

A buck deer, ragged shreds of velvet still clinging to his antlers, passed within thirty feet and never knew Sean was there. A mink, come to hunt fingerling trout, flashed like a brown shadow along the pool, totally unaware of him. Even a keen-eyed, red-tailed hawk, circling the mud flat for what it could see and pick up, did not detect the big Setter.

All through the day, all night long, and half through the next morning, Sean lay in the mud. Then, his fever gone, he was aroused by a sudden flutter of wings.

A bittern dipped out of the sky, alighted in the swamp, stood a moment, and then, with the extreme slowness of motion that marks its kind, it began to walk toward Sean. Less than two yards away, beside a cluster of reeds that grew near the pond, it took its stance. Bill pointed toward the sky, brown-feathered wings folded and motionless, it looked almost like one of the reeds. The bittern never shifted a feather as it waited for some unwary prey to venture within reach of its spear-like bill.

Sean watched, his eyes wide open. He felt better, and with a return of physical well-being had come the return of hunger. Never in his life had he seen a bittern, but he suspected that they might be good to eat.

With a sudden leap he was out of the mud and flinging himself toward the waiting bird. For a split second the startled bittern did not move, and that mistake was its last. Had it taken to the air instantly,

Sean could not have caught it. As it was, the dog overtook the fluttering bird four feet out over the pond and both went under the water.

Sean carried his victim back to the mud flat and shook himself. Water and mud flew in all directions. The big Setter felt a great, glowing pride in this, the first game he had ever caught. He dropped the limp bittern on the mud, snuffled it, and pawed it. Experimentally he touched it with his tongue, and sneezed when a feather tickled his nose. Again he took the bittern in his mouth and trotted toward high ground.

He sat down, head cocked forward and ears pricked up. Now that he finally had something to eat, the next problem was just how to go about eating it. Definitely the feathers were not to his taste. Sean rolled the bittern over with his paw. Then, as though an idea had just occurred to him, he held the bird down with both front paws and used his teeth to pluck the feathers out. As soon as he had stripped a portion he ate it, and went back for another. Five minutes later only the bird's bill and feathers remained in the huckleberry thicket. Sean was so ravenous that he ate even the feet and head.

He looked about him. For the second time since leaving Danny's clearing he had eaten. But, like the mushrooms, the bittern had merely dulled the sharpest edges of his appetite. He felt a great need for more food.

Aimlessly he wandered up a ridge. Though he was famished, he hadn't the least idea of how to go about getting something more to eat. Except for the bittern, and his games with the mouse in his kennel, never in his life had he hunted anything. Though he had

already received some lessons in woods lore, he had
not yet learned how to apply them.

Unless he did he would die. All his life Sean had
been pampered and cared for. Now he must take care
of himself; the wild world has no place for the weak
or incompetent. Only the fit and knowing survive.

Sean's neck and shoulder still pained a little, but
they no longer burned and hurt as fiercely as they
had. He limped slightly as he prowled up the
hardwood ridge, snuffling at the various scents about
him. All were interesting and some were tempting,
but Sean did not know what he could do about any of
them. He saw nothing except a few birds that flitted
out of reach.

Suddenly a rabbit exploded from a patch of grass
and raced away, white tail flashing like a powder
puff. Sean gave instant, determined chase. But the
cottontail dived into a burrow, a safe twenty jumps
ahead of the dog. Sean sniffed the warm odors that
wafted out of the burrow, and scratched hopefully at
its mouth, but the cottontail knew a safe refuge. This
burrow was strategically placed between two almost
buried boulders. Not even a bear could dig into it
and only a weasel or mink could enter.

After a few minutes Sean wandered despondently
on. His shriveled stomach cried for food, but there
was none. Coming to a patch of wintergreen, Sean
plucked and ate as many of the tangy red berries as
he could find. They were as nothing to his hunger.

He was drooling now, and desperately turning
aside for anything that might be edible. Again he
dashed at a rabbit and again failed to catch it. Hopefully he reared against a tree in which a fat por-

cupine, rendered safe by his sharp spears and scornful of everything that was not so protected, dwelt in philosophic seclusion. Unaware of his good fortune because he had discovered the porcupine in a tree and had not overtaken it and tried to kill it on the ground, Sean wandered on.

The sun was swinging toward its bed behind the western mountains when Sean halted abruptly. A most enticing odor crossed his nostrils. The dog bent his head into the wind that brought him the scent, and ran out an appreciative tongue.

He smelled fresh meat in ample quantities, but mingled with it was another odor that made Sean bristle. Never before had he detected an odor similar to this one. It was like a dog's, but it was not dog. There was something about it that was almost evil.

Sean had caught the scent of Slasher, who was neither dog nor coyote but half of each, and one of Slasher's kills.

The big Setter hesitated. The kill was not his and under ordinary circumstances he would have passed it by. Now he was too hungry to ignore anything that might be good to eat. He trotted forward, halted, and advanced a few more steps. Throwing caution and discretion to the winds, he flung himself toward the food that he knew lay just a few steps ahead of him.

In a little opening among the trees, where Slasher had finally pulled her down this morning, lay a dead whitetail doe. The skin was ripped from her belly, and there was a knife-clean cut where Slasher had gone in to get the liver, the part of a fresh kill that he liked best. Nothing else was touched.

Trembling with excitement and hunger, Sean sank

his fangs deep into red meat, ripped out a great
chunk, and swallowed it whole. He continued to eat,
filling his belly as fast as he could without regard to
anything else. Only when the hunger pangs had
started to quiet did he make any effort to select only
the tenderest and best parts of the slain doe.

Now he went about it a little more carefully and
not quite so hastily. For the first time since leaving
Danny he had enough to eat. Sean raised his head to
lick his chops, then selected another morsel.

Suddenly he became aware that he was no longer
alone. The big Setter raised his head to look across
the clearing. Fifteen feet away, Slasher faced him.

Product of a big mongrel dog and a female coyote,
the coy-dog had inherited the size of his father and
the lithe grace of his mother. His fur was long and
gray, except for brindle stripes, his father's markings,
down both sides. His muzzle tapered like a wolf's,
but there was a certain squareness about it, and a
certain fuzziness, that again bespoke Slasher's
mixed parentage.

His eyes were clear yellow, and in them seemed to
glitter the hate that a hybrid, who could claim no
family as his own, felt for the entire world. Slasher
was a born killer, a perennial pirate who had so far
been too clever to be caught and punished for his
misdeeds. In spite of the fact that, on occasion, he led
a pack of renegade dogs through the hills, most of the
time he preferred to be alone. Slasher had simmered
in the juices of his own hatred for so long that not
even the few mates he had tried to take could for long
put up with him.

He edged in to kill the red Setter.

Sean rose to defend himself, and there was no fear in him. Slasher was as big as he, and constant running in the wilds had developed his muscles to a hardness and flexibility that Sean had yet to achieve. In addition, there were few tricks of battle that Slasher did not know. Sean did not realize this. He only knew that here was an enemy who must be faced.

With a haste born of overconfidence, Slasher sprang in for the kill. Sean braced himself to meet the attack, and Slasher stopped short. Like a dancer, he glided safely away.

He had thought to make a plaything of Sean, and to chop him to pieces at his will. Most of the dogs Slasher had killed had been easy victims. Some fought for a little while, some tried to run, but all feared him. Now, for the first time, he met a dog that was not afraid of him and that had no intention of running. Slasher ran out a dripping tongue while he studied his opponent.

Again he dived in, snapped, and the end half-inch of Sean's left ear hung by bloody shreds. Slasher feinted to the left, crossed suddenly to the right, and made a tentative snap at Sean's throat. Of one thing Slasher was positive. He could kill this strange dog, this creature who smelled of man but not of fear, at any moment he chose.

Suddenly, for no reason that was at once apparent, Slasher whirled, streaked into a thicket, and faded like a flitting shadow. Sean, whose senses were not as keen as those of the wilderness-trained coy-dog, stood still for a moment. Then the odor that had sent Slasher flying was also borne to him.

A man was coming and it was nobody Sean knew. Therefore he had better go, too. A single prodigious leap carried him into the surrounding trees, but, unlike Slasher, he did not run fast. He knew men, and was aware of the fact that no man could match the pace of a dog that wanted to travel at even moderate speed. Two hundred yards from the dead doe, safely screened by trees and brush, Sean slowed to a walk.

His nose told him when the man, who was Jake Busher's neighbor, came to the dead doe and halted beside it. Then the man went on.

Sean shook his lacerated ear and tried to lick off the flecks of blood. The interrupted fight had ended with no conclusive victory, though probably Slasher would have won had it continued. He was hard and wise, more than a match for any ordinary dog his own size. Nevertheless Sean remained unafraid. He was entirely willing to fight Slasher again should their paths cross.

Sean sought a high, sun-baked ridge, and slept. The night air roused him and restlessly he started prowling again. Exercise revived his hunger and he cast about for something to eat. He jumped at and missed three rabbits, sniffed hopefully at a tree in which a brood of wild turkeys roosted, and stood rooted in surprise when a big raccoon, prowling among some trees, fluffed its fur to twice its normal size, spat at him, and scampered up a tree. Sean reared against the tree's trunk, snuffling long and deeply of this new scent. It was tempting, and one he would have to remember.

Dawn had come again, and still Sean had eaten

nothing, when he thought of the dead doe. He knew that Slasher might be there too, but Sean remained unafraid of Slasher. At a distance-eating trot he set off toward the place where the doe lay. From a safe distance he stopped to reconnoiter.

The scent of the doe was very plain, as was that of the man who had passed it. There was only yesterday's evidence of Slasher. Sean dismissed the coydog from his mind while he gave his attention to what lay at hand. He wrinkled his nose distastefully.

There was something present that had not been here before, something more cold, more deadly, and, if possible, more evil than Slasher himself. Sean trembled. Then he heard the faint voice of a sick crow, and slunk forward. Whatever might be present he must discover before he was discovered by it. Carefully he edged through the trees and looked at the place where the dead doe lay.

As he did so a scavenger crow launched itself feebly from the carcass, rose ten feet, made a complete somersault, and fell to the ground. It jerked a convulsive wing as it landed, and then only the breeze ruffled its feathers. Three more dead crows lay close to the deer. Sean smelled only the odor of man, and knew it was the same man who had interrupted his fight with Slasher. But he continued to shiver.

There was something here that he could not figure out, a fearful, deadly something that had no foundation whatever in the logic of his nose. He bristled up to the kill, sniffed at it and at the three dead crows. Then Sean turned his attention to the fourth crow, the one he had watched fall to the ground. It was still warm, the animal heat having not yet gone from its body, but it was certainly dead. Again Sean sniffed at the doe, but all he could discover was that the man, in passing, had paused near it.

Finally Sean's hunger overcame prudence and he ripped off and swallowed a chunk of meat. He champed his jaws, not liking the taste, and almost at once was violently ill. There was a fierce burning in his stomach and a throbbing in his head. He staggered, and was ill again.

Shakily, unsteadily, he walked away from the dead doe to the cool shade of a nearby hemlock. Overcome by nausea, he lay down. Both lying still and walking were unbearable. Sean rose to stagger on. Sides heaving violently, he stretched his full length on the ground.

He could not know that the hill man, looking for a runaway heifer, had found the doe, recognized it as a dog or wolf kill, and poisoned it. Slasher, like so many wolves and coyotes, knew better than to return to a kill after a man had discovered it. Sean had learned the hard way. It was his good fortune that, in the chunk of meat he had chosen, there was a heavy overdose of strychnine. Instead of killing Sean by being absorbed, it had made him so ill that he had promptly rid himself of it. He was left with nothing more serious than a severe nausea.

That passed, leaving him with a hot tongue and a throbbing head. Sean rose, walked slowly to a little spring he had found, and drank. Very tired, he sought the sunny top of a hillock and curled up to sleep.

A sure sense, an inborn knowledge that something was around, awakened him. But Sean did not move.

The games he had taught himself back in the kennel run were well-taught. Not for nothing had he learned that a motionless object is hardest to see. A scent tickled his nostrils, and a moment later Sean found the source of the odor with his eyes.

Four feet away, its back to Sean, a cottontail rabbit was placidly chewing clover. Sean launched himself as he had at the bittern, and, in his kennel, at the mouse. From a recumbent position he went up and out. The startled rabbit made one frantic jump, but Sean's leap had been perfect. His jaws snapped once and the rabbit quivered in them.

Thus, finally, he learned a priceless lesson. The bittern had alighted near him while he lay buried in the mud. The cottontail had ventured close as he lay sleeping. So Sean learned the value and some of the technique of an ambush. It was better, and easier, to let game come to him than it was to waste his strength running after it.

He had found food, but he remained terribly lonely, yearning for companionship. It was loneliness that, two days later, sent him back to Jake Busher's clearing. From the safe shelter of the forest Sean looked out on the cabin and corral. He danced with his front feet and whined, wanting to be near the man but not daring to go. Jake Busher's shotgun and the poisoned doe had taught him well the wisdom of being careful in choosing his friends.

Black night fell before he ventured into the clearing at last. He sat there, in no hurry to go near the house until the light winked out and Jake went to bed. Cautious as he was, Sean could not resist creeping up to the cabin and sniffing it. His tail began to wag as he recalled happy memories of the many fine times he had enjoyed with men.

All around the cabin he went, snuffling long and hard at everything. He did not even overlook a chip of wood that Jake Busher had touched. Finally Sean went from the cabin to the corral, where the sheep stared back stupidly as he peered between the corral rails at them.

Sean bristled as a new scent came to him, and looked anxiously at the house. Under no circumstances did he want Jake Busher to find out that he was in the clearing, and Jake might if a fight started there. Sean trotted back toward the forest.

Across the clearing, creeping ever nearer to the corralled sheep, came Slasher.

5. Penny

Jake Busher, sleeping in his cabin, was awakened by the stuttering bawl of a terrified sheep. Without lingering to hear any more, the hill man leaped from his bed, groped in the darkness for his clothing, slipped his feet into moccasins, and padded silently across the cabin's floor.

This was an act which, in his mind, he had rehearsed many times. He knew the raider that came out of the forest as a devilishly clever brute, a creature crafty beyond belief. As silently as a ghost it struck at his flock and at the flocks and herds of his neighbors, and just as stealthily it was gone. Its technique varied. Sheep and calves that ranged the far-flung hill pastures were often found in their isolated ranges with their throats slashed or their bellies ripped. But by no means did the killer confine itself to open range. Sometimes, as it was doing now, it ventured right up to a house and launched its attack. Nor did it always come by night. On occasion when a hill man went away he was apt to return and find that his livestock had been raided in broad daylight and within sight of a cabin. The killer seemed possessed of an almost supernatural intelligence. Never did it show itself about a clearing in daylight if man was present.

In the black night Jake reached for his shotgun, loaded with buckshot this time, and for a powerful torch which he had walked twenty miles to buy. The torch, of the newest and latest make, would shoot a dazzling white beam a thousand feet and focus on whatever might be around. The light had cost Jake a great deal of money that he could ill afford to spend, and he had bought it solely to have such a light around if the killer came to his clearing at night.

Out in the darkness all the sheep were bawling now. Jake heard the patter of running hooves and a sharp thud as some luckless animal flung itself against the corral. But Jake did not hurry. Bitter personal experience had taught him the craft and cunning of the raider. Only a man who was equally crafty and cunning could hope to get a fair shot at it.

Very slowly, careful not to make a sound, Jake walked to the cabin's door, lifted the latch, and opened the door. He had prepared for this, too. The door latch and hinges were kept so well-greased that they could be moved and worked without the slightest squeak.

A step at a time, knowing exactly where to place his feet so no squeaky or creaking board would betray him, Jake went out onto his covered porch. Only when he stood on the outer edge, where he had ample room to swing his gun without danger of interference, did he stop.

The corralled sheep were bleating and bawling a nightmarish, discordant medley of terror. Jake brought the shotgun to his shoulder, slipped the safety catch, and with his left hand raised the torch so that its beam would point where the shotgun was pointing. He lighted the torch.

Dazzling white light stabbed the darkness and held the corral and part of the barn in its brilliant beam. The sheep, still bleating and bawling, had retreated to one end of the corral and bunched there, as though they would somehow find safety in their very numbers.

Jake swore under his breath. Careful as he had been, the raider had outwitted him. Probably he had betrayed himself by some unintentional sound too faint for human ears, but loud enough for the keen ears of the night-raiding pirate. In any event, there was nothing in the corral except sheep. Jake criss-crossed the clearing with his torch. He swore again, loudly this time, centered the ivory bead of his shotgun on a running creature that was just leaping into the forest, and pressed the trigger. The shotgun belched its leaden buckshot and Jake pressed the other trigger to shoot the left barrel.

The shots were fired more in frustration and rage than for any practical reason. Even as he shot the first time, Jake knew that his target was already safe among the trees. Nevertheless there was a faint hope that he might hit something, and Jake fired the second barrel because of that hope.

He reloaded his shotgun and stood still for a moment, cold fury distorting his face. He had not brought the raider down but he had seen it. For the second time he had seen it.

It was a big, red dog, doubtless the same that, a few days ago, had come openly into his clearing. At that time, never suspecting that a raider as clever as this one would come in broad daylight, Jake had had his shotgun loaded with bird shot. Mourning doves came into the clearing every evening, and Jake had had a light load because he hoped to get a couple. He knew he had stung the dog with bird shot, but he hadn't expected to kill it with such a load.

Obviously it was a bold devil, crafty and fearless, and more than slightly contemptuous of the men from whom it took such a high tribute. Jake felt a cold shiver tremble up his spine. Such a beast, too familiar with men, might not hesitate to kill a man should circumstances demand it. Maybe it had even come back to attack his sheep for revenge. The thought inspired more than a little fear.

Jake left the porch and lighted his way down to the corral. He played the light over the frightened sheep, then on the trampled floor of the corral. Another explosive oath ripped from his lips. Three sheep lay where they had fallen, their throats sliced cleanly and their blood flowing into dark puddles under the light. A little wind moved their bedraggled wool.

Fiercely Jake swung back toward the forest. Every inch of the trees bordering the clearing he searched with the torch while his finger itched on the shotgun's trigger. Then, finding nothing, he turned to the task at hand. If the dead sheep received prompt attention he could send them to market early tomorrow morning. He himself would not go. There was a score to settle and, as he worked over his murdered stock, Jack swore a solemn oath that he would settle that score.

When the dressed and skinned sheep were properly hung in the cool night air, Jake stretched out to spend what remained of the night near his corral.

He awoke with the first glow of morning. Unless he could watch them every minute, he did not dare let the corralled sheep loose to forage for themselves. If they were not safe in the corral, they were in ten times as much danger out in the clearings or in the forest. Jake threw them some hay that he had cut to supply his stock through the bitter winter that lay just ahead, made himself some breakfast, and, with the shotgun under his arm, set off along a foot path.

Twenty minutes later he was at the clearing of Tobe Miller, his nearest neighbor. Tobe put down his axe and came forward to greet him.

"Howdy, Jake."

"Mornin', Tobe."

Tobe Miller grinned. "What you loaded for? Bear?"

Jake shook his head. "Dog."

"Dog?"

"That's right! Red dog nigh as big as a yearlin' calf! He got three of my sheep last night! I saw him! 'Tain't a wolf at all that's been cuttin' our stock down!"

"I'll be jugged! Could of swore it was a wolf! I run across one of his kills up in the back lands and it sure looked to me like a wolf kill! I poisoned it."

"It's a dog," Jake said positively. "I saw him. Tobe, we got to kill him or we won't have nothin' left!"

"We got to get him," Tobe admitted. "But how?"

"Put every man as can handle a gun into the hills

and hunt him down. If we can't do that, maybe we can run him out."

"Might work," Tobe conceded.

"It's got to work. I'm goin' to see the Prentices, the Carters, and the Allens. Think Rose would hitch up and take my three sheep into Cottstown for me? They're butchered and hangin' near the barn."

"I'm sure she would," Tobe assured him. "I'll cut into the hills myself as soon as I've had somethin' to eat. I'll beat the brush up around Forks Valley. Come eat with us?"

"No thanks. I'll be gettin' on."

Jake visited the three clearings of which he had spoken, and told his story. At each clearing one or more gaunt hill men, who knew from firsthand experience the difficulty of just earning a living on their rocky, rough farms, listened attentively. These were men who understood completely the seriousness of having a stock killer loose, and they also knew the ways of animals. All agreed to join in the hunt for Sean, and they divided the country so that there was no nearby section which would not be thoroughly covered by at least one expert huntsman.

Jake hurried back to his own clearing. He knew exactly where he had watched Sean enter the forest last night, and went to that place. The trees and nearby brush were scored and torn where the buckshot had ripped through them, but there was no blood. Jake gave a moment to deep thought.

He would know how to look for a wolf, but a dog turned outlaw was a different problem. He might be anywhere. There was no hope of tracking on the snowless ground, and therefore the only thing to do was look everywhere.

Jake swung up a ridge, traveling fast because it was an aspen ridge with few thickets and almost no cover. The raiding dog was very cunning; there was little chance that he would go where he would not find cover. When he came to a brush-grown valley, Jake proceeded more cautiously. He saw five deer, a brood of grouse, numerous rabbits, and even surprised a wild turkey on the ground. But there was no dog or even any dog tracks. That evening Jake returned to his clearing.

Early the next morning he was out again. He combed every ridge, every valley, and every thicket in the territory assigned to him and still did not see a dog. On the third day he jumped a coyote out of a little draw and brought it down with one shot.

Nor did the rest come any nearer to bagging a big, red dog, although the Carter men brought in three coyotes and Tobe Miller shot a lynx. Not one hunter had had so much as one look at Sean. On the night of the fourth day, all the hunters gathered at Tobe Miller's house. Nobody was sure as to what they should do next, but young Price Allen offered a constructive suggestion.

"Maybe he's gone," he said. "It's all right with me if he has. I can't afford to lose another calf. If he hasn't gone, and comes back to kill again, we'll get him sure when snow flies. Gives us a chance to track him, or set a hound pack on his trail on snow so we know where they're goin', and he won't get away."

High on a timbered ridge, Sean slept peacefully with his head curled against his silken flank. It was not a haphazard or ill-chosen position, certainly not the sleeping place Sean might have selected a week before. All about him huge pines, their pitch-sticky trunks bare of limbs for thirty feet or more, waved green branches that whispered quietly high above him. Beneath the big trees was a cluster of young pines from two to five feet high and with limbs that grew almost to the needle-littered ground. It was in the small pines that Sean bedded. Nothing on the ground could see him unless he chose to be seen.

The bed had another advantage. The winds, which were beginning to lose their summery warmth, swirled all about the little pines. Not only was Sean himself well-hidden and sheltered, but the various breezes would bring him warning of anything that might care to seek him out.

Two hundred yards down the slope, a pair of antlered bucks, half in play and half in earnest, parried and thrust with their antlers. Before very long, when the mating season was fully upon them and the real battle for does began, the same two bucks would battle until the smaller flung himself away, perhaps with a long-tined antler deep in his chest.

Just over the rim of the slope, rabbits played about, and high in one of the pines a coal-black squirrel jumped from sturdy branch to swaying twig as he practiced new aerial maneuvers. The squirrel, a creature which fascinated Sean, lived in the pines but made long trips to the bordering beeches in order to collect and store his winter's supply of food.

Sean twitched in his sleep, aware without awakening that a new creature had come upon the scene and was within scenting distance. It was a black and white heifer, the same one Tobe Miller had been trailing when he found and poisoned the doe's carcass. For centuries all the heifer's ancestors had been gentle, barn-abiding creatures that lived and died solely to serve the needs of man. But the seeds of wildness, after a lapse of many generations, had sprouted anew in the heifer. She could stand nothing of restraint, neither four walls nor pasture. Now, wild as any elk and just as crafty, she lived the never-hampered but always-perilous life of a wild creature. But, unlike Sean, she had chosen it voluntarily.

Suddenly awakened, Sean raised his head and glared suspiciously about. He was annoyed and slightly nervous; even while he slept he thought he knew everything about him, and yet he had been struck on the head by some light object. The Setter glanced up into the nearest pine, hid his irritation, and yawned widely to prove that he had never really been bothered at all.

Teetering on a limb was Silverwing, the raven. Bigger than a crow, and shaggy instead of sleek, Silverwing had come by his local name because of the three bright, silver feathers that gleamed in his black wing. About to drop another pine cone on Sean's head, Silverwing chortled and chuckled because the first had been effective. A master of the practical joke, Silverwing knew very well that the first cone had alarmed the big Setter, and he was gleeful about it.

From off in the forest came three rasping caws and Silverwing flew away as silently as he had come. His mate, having found food, was calling him and she would not eat until he came.

Sean rose, yawned, and stretched. He looked off in the direction Silverwing had taken, still faintly annoyed. But there were too many things of the present for Sean to concern himself with the past or future.

That night he had lingered in Jake Busher's clearing long enough to see Slasher attack the sheep and kill three. Then he had seen the coy-dog's hasty departure and Jake's light, and let both serve as a warning to himself. But when he ran from the clearing, with the sound of tearing and thudding buckshot to speed him on his way, Sean had not run very far.

He had gone to the nearest rabbit thicket, and there he had ambushed and eaten another rabbit. Prowling through the night, he had lain up in a different thicket when daylight came. Twice that day had Jake Busher passed within feet of him without seeing him or even suspecting that he was near. Thus did Sean prove his possession of qualities which no completely wild creature owns.

Slasher, or any experienced wolf or fox, would have smelled the man coming and slunk out ahead of him without being seen. An inexperienced beast might have waited until Jake was very near, then broken, run, and offered Jake a good shot. But Sean had stayed right where he was, never moving at all. None knew better than he that men had great and mysterious powers at their command; what besides man could reach out and injure a thing that he could not personally touch? But when it came to woodcraft, the keenest man could not compare to the dullest wild creature.

After that there had been more hunters. Four times had Sean lain without moving while a man who would have taken his life passed less than a stone's throw away. Not once had he been discovered.

But the invasion by armed huntsmen had proven too much for Slasher's hair-trigger nerves. Sean had run across his day-old trail near the head of Forks Valley, and again three miles farther north. Slasher was leaving, at least until the hornets' nest which he himself had stirred up quieted down and he could safely return.

Sean left the little pines, walked to the edge of the slope, and felt up-blowing air fresh and cold in his face. Nothing on the hillside had changed except that the sparring bucks had broken apart and gone their separate ways. Sean stopped to snuffle the place where they had been.

A growing uneasiness and a dismal sense of loneliness sat heavily upon him. Sean had never been born to walk alone. Unlike Slasher, who was entirely self-sufficient and who thought of and needed only himself, Sean alone could never be happy. He needed someone or something to share the lavish love that he had to spare. Hungry, but not caring to hunt, he padded uneasily back and forth on the side of the slope.

There was a rustling, a cracking of brush, and Tobe Miller's runaway heifer rose from her bed to look belligerently at him. The runaway, fully aware of her own size and strength, had no intention of hiding from anything as small as a dog. She shook her horns threateningly and made a short little charge. Sean ducked sideways into the brush and loped away from her. He had no quarrel with the heifer. It never occurred to him that he could or should hunt anything so big. He just felt that he would be better off if he avoided her.

The heifer went back to the thicket to chew her cud and to switch the few flies and gnats that had not yet been driven into hiding or killed by frosts. Sean continued to cast nervously back and forth. He was still hungry, but lack of company provided a more heartfelt ache than lack of food.

A big buck, its neck faintly swollen as a sign that the rut, or mating season, was about to begin, moved slowly out of his way, then stopped to glare at him. Sean paid no attention.

Night fell, and the unsatisfied longing within him became more intense. He sat down on a rocky ledge that overlooked a deep valley, thrust his tail straight out behind him, adjusted his front paws, pointed his muzzle at the sky, and wailed his heartbreak to the wilderness.

Rising to a high crescendo, and dying away in a series of sobbing little noises, his mournful dirge rolled forth. On a faraway hillside a hunting fox paused to listen, and knew the sound for what it was. The fox went on with his hunt. His own mate was safe; somewhere on the hillside and not too far away she was hunting, too. Neither the fox nor his mate could concern themselves with a lone, luckless dog.

When he had finished his song Sean felt better, and descended to the valley. There a good-sized creek, low from the summer's drought and not yet replenished by the autumn rains, wove a tenuous way around sun-baked rocks or gathered itself in placid pools. Sean had discovered three days ago that some of the pools, shallow and almost land-locked, contained fat suckers that had no place to go except the length and width of the pool. He had found that he could catch the suckers.

Unhesitatingly he plunged in, sending a great splash of water high into the air and watching through fading ripples as a school of suckers swam away from him. Sean flung himself on the ripples and snapped at shadowy fish that flitted past on both sides. His jaws found and clamped on a two-pound sucker. He ate.

After his meal he felt the urge to run, and he lengthened out to fly along the stream bed. His wild race became a sort of mad flight. Heedless of any-thing save the wind that lashed his face, he left the water course to race straight up a mountain. Though his tongue lolled and he was exercise-warmed, he did not stop to drink.

Pressed by a great urgency to do or find something, Sean himself was not sure what he sought. He re-laxed his run into a mile-eating trot, but hour after hour, stopping for nothing and always traveling in a perfectly straight line, he flew along. The night was half spent when he became aware that he was ap-proaching a human habitation.

He stopped short, tested the winds, and advanced at a walk. This was no hill man's clearing and shack, but broad and cultivated acres much like the Haggin estate. Sean drank in the odors of cattle, horses, and sheep. He savored the scent of men and dogs. Cautiously the big Setter trotted out of the forest and into the clearing.

Only night lights glowed in the big house and about the barns and tenant houses, and at best they cast only a feeble glow. The people who were active about this house by day had been driven by night to the comfort and safety of their beds. Sean tested all the odors again and again, hoping to find one he knew. There was none.

Unafraid, knowing by instinct and from recent experience that the night is a friendly protector of the fugitive and the hunted, Sean padded across a meadow and onto a velvet lawn. Suddenly homesick, he whined uneasily. Many times had he trotted across a lawn exactly like this one. Keeping out of the glow of the night lights, he went to the tenant houses and sniffed them carefully.

Totally unaware of the fact that, by accident, he had reached Jordan Acres, the place he would have gone anyway had not his crate fallen out of the truck, Sean left the tenant houses for the big house. He ventured onto the porch, heedless of the fact that his dew-wet paws left muddy prints, and thoroughly investigated everything about it.

Somewhere in the house a man coughed in his sleep. Sean froze where he was and did not move again until he was sure that the man was not chasing him. He trotted toward the dog kennels.

Vaguely visible in the night, a white and black English Setter stalked stiffly down to the end of his run, thrust his muzzle against the wire, and sniffed noses with Sean. Sean met him as stiffly, but after they became acquainted two tails began to wag. The

English Setter by wriggling his body invited Sean to frolic.

A sudden overwhelming scent jerked Sean's head sidewise. He lifted his front paw, like a bird dog on a point, and stood very quiet for ten seconds. He shook his head to clear a bit of dust from his nose, and ran his tongue out. Sean whined softly. At a slow but steady walk he began to move along the row of kennels.

Other dogs came in the night to meet him. Most were suspicious, alert, as though there clung to Sean something that the rest of them did not have. But there was no growl or snarl and only normal barks; the dogs were ready to fight or be friendly. Sean passed them by, all his senses concentrated on the one scent that had lured him. He came to the end of the row of kennels and stood transfixed.

She stood inside her wire run, alert and trembling. Not coweringly, but expectantly, her tail drooped in a graceful curve. Even in the dim starlight her gorgeous coat shimmered and reflected a soft glow. There she stood, Penelope of Killarney. One of the most wonderful of her wonderful breed, Penny had been Sean's appointed mate. Taut as a fiddle string, she watched him sidle gently toward her.

Gone was Sean's loneliness and the uneasy feeling that he was deserted. Staring hard at Penny, his tail wagged stiffly. He bounced forward, holding his legs rigid like those of a mechanical toy. Then he began to wag everything behind his nose. Sean pressed hard against the wire and a pleading little whine broke from him.

She came slowly, so taut and so tense that her slim

flanks fluttered and her pounding heart could be heard. Through the wire she sniffed noses with him, and her tail started to wag.

Sean did a gallant little dance, tail high over his back and ears alerted. He pirouetted and came back to her.

She stooped, hind quarters in the air and front feet stretched on the ground in front of her. Dashing madly away, she raced at top speed to the end of her kennel run and flew back. Suddenly coy, she stopped five feet from the wire, where he could not reach her.

Sean barked at her, a sharp and pleading little sound that again brought her close. He poked at the unyielding wire with his big front paw. Then, with a warm, wet tongue, he licked as much of her face as he could reach through the wire mesh.

Dawn was in the sky before he would leave her side to hide himself in the forest. He loved this place, so like his old home, and he would gladly have stayed. Had there been anyone around that he knew, he would have stayed. But there were only strangers.

Bitter experience had taught Sean not to trust them.

6. Hound Pack

For a full two weeks Sean kept close to Tom Jordan's estate. By day he lay up on one of the beech ridges, but he spent every night outside of Penny's run. During those two weeks the weather underwent a radical change.

The big beech trees, that had started dropping their podded nuts shortly after the first frost, shed their leaves, too. The wind at night was always cold and even at mid-day there was a cold tang in the air. Almost every night there was a hard freeze, so that ice formed around the edges of the shallower pools and quieter streams.

Sean had easy hunting during this last great feast before snow covered the wilderness and brought empty bellies to the forest dwellers. Squirrels by the hundred were busy from dawn to dark gathering and storing fallen beechnuts. Shuffling black bears, deer, raccoons, chipmunks, all creatures that wanted to eat the ripe nuts, came to the beech forests to have their fill. Four-footed and feathered meat-eaters, not interested in the nuts themselves, gathered to take their toll of the gentler creatures that were in the woods to harvest.

It was there that Sean learned to hunt and catch grouse. A born bird dog, numberless times he had stalked grouse and tried to catch them. Always they had drummed away before he came even close. But the grouse that came to the beech woods, and there were dozens of them, stuffed their crops so full that their chests were swollen like pouter pigeons and they were reluctant to fly. Instead they preferred simply to walk out of the way. Much of the time a quick sidewise jump and one snap of the jaws would result in a capture.

For the first time since his crate spilled out the back end of the truck, Sean was contented. No longer restless, he had no urge to roam. Penny's companionship filled the gnawing void of loneliness that was so difficult to bear.

Well-fed and warm, Sean burrowed a little farther into the pile of leaves which he had chosen for his bed and tucked his black nose a little deeper into his warm flank. The wind that keened out of the valley was a sharp one with a real bite in its teeth. Since early morning the sky had been shrouded in a blanket of ominous black clouds, and a few snowflakes had pattered down. Frost glittered on the north side of all the trees.

Protected by his heavy coat, Sean felt none of the wind's bitterness or the frost's numbing chill. Born in the Wintapi anyhow, and recently conditioned by running wild, he cared little what the bitterest weather could offer. Sean could live through a cold snap that might leave a short-haired dog frozen in its bed.

The pattering snow fell faster, rattling crisply against the shriveled beech leaves as it struck. Sean's red fur was speckled with white, and finally covered completely, as two inches of the season's first snowfall piled up in the beech woods. Sean slept on, uncaring. The snow covering him served as an insulating blanket, and he was warmer than he would have been without it.

Toward evening the snow stopped, leaving a three-inch fall in the forest. Sean rose from his bed, shook himself prodigiously, and in the space of half a second he transformed his white coat back into Irish Setter red. He stood a moment, testing the winds to find what lay about, then started down the slope.

The snow had interfered only partially with the bustling activity of the numerous hungry creatures who had come to feast on the beechnuts. Sean passed a craggy-horned buck, somber in his gray winter coat, who was pawing through snow and leaves alike and licking up the tiny nuts he exposed. Squirrels scurried back and forth. Striped chipmunks, their cheek pouches filled to the bursting point, dived into holes and crevices to add to the store of food they had already hidden.

Only the grouse were gone, driven by this first snow to the warmth of evergreen thickets where they huddled unhappily. Later they would emerge and until spring would eke out a precarious existence on buds, bittersweet, frozen rose hips, and whatever else they were able to find. Grouse did not like the first snow because they knew too well what would follow.

Turning aside for nothing, his eagerness to see Penny overcoming his hunger, Sean cut a straight course down the slope. Lights glowed in the tenant cabins and the big house, and the pungent odor of burning logs hung heavily in the air. Sean did not hesitate. Shortly after he came the first time he had learned that almost never were the kennels visited after dark. There was really no need for visiting them. The kennel men saw to it that everything was in order before they retired, and should anything go amiss the dogs themselves would give warning.

Careful only to keep out of the golden light that escaped through unshaded windows, Sean went directly to the kennels. He paused to sniff noses with the big English Setter, and with a few more dogs along the way. Grown used to his visits, sure of his friendly intentions, they did not snarl or even bark now when he came. Sean increased his walk to a trot. A little whining sound of joy escaped him.

She was not only there to meet him, but the snow at the end of her kennel run was trampled and scuffed where she had awaited his visit for two hours. Her tail wagged a happy greeting and she came at once to press her cold nose against the steel wire. When she gave, Penny gave her whole heart. She was just as anxious for Sean's visits as he was to see her.

They pressed very close together while Sean whimpered softly to her. He sat down, plumed tail straight behind him and as close to the wire as he could get. Penny licked his lacerated ear, the souvenir of his fight with Slasher. She whirled to race along the wire run, inviting him to frolic, and he accepted her invitation. For two hours, while the lights in the various houses slowly winked out, they romped and played. Side by side they lay down, but there was still the wire between them.

Sean had studied the wire from every angle. He had bitten it with his teeth, poked it with his paws, brushed against it, and tried to push through it. The wire was the only thin barrier between himself and his love. But it might as well have been a brick wall ten feet thick, for he did not know how to break it down or how to bring Penny completely to his side.

The black autumn night was giving way to the late autumn dawn when he unwillingly left her side and returned to the beech woods. Had he been sure of a welcome from the human beings around the place, he might have stayed. But Sean had had too many harsh lessons from men to trust any of them. There was no promise that the men who lived at Jordan Acres would receive him with any more kindness than Jake Busher had shown. He dared not take a chance.

Veering away from his bed of the day before, Sean entered a thicket of beech brush. The bigger trees, bare of leaves, were gaunt and naked against the cold sky. But crisp leaves still clung tenaciously to the lower beech brush, and would cling there until they were finally banished by the new foliage of spring. Sean went into the thicket hoping to find game, but by luck he was spared even the necessity of hunting his own breakfast.

Just outside the thicket a feeding rabbit made a wild dash for safety as a cruising hawk struck him. The rabbit came within a split hair of reaching shelter, for at the very edge of the thicket the hawk had to let go or risk colliding with a beech sapling. But the hawk's sharp claws had already done their work. Tumbling end over end, propelled by its own momentum, the rabbit died within six feet of Sean.

At once he sprang up to claim it, and was standing over his prize when the hawk recovered himself and turned back for the rabbit. The hawk glared at Sean, the thief who had taken his dinner. But he could do little except snap his mandibles and fly away. Sean ate and lay down to sleep.

The sun was still low in the eastern sky when he jerked his head erect. The winds brought him the scent of two men, and Sean knew that they were two who lived at Jordan Acres. They were still strangers to him, and no stranger had good intentions. Sean kept his head up, following with his nose the progress of the pair.

They came nearer. The sound of their footsteps was plain in the crisp air and their voices carried clearly.

"Don't shoot it, just find it, Jordan says," one of the men remarked sarcastically. "Could be Haggin's Irish Setter. Hah!"

"Yeah," the second man snorted. "Can you imagine one of them oversize lap hounds livin' this long without anybody to tend him? Haggin's dog has been dead this good while. For my money this is some wild hound that's been livin' in the woods and took a shine to Penny."

"That's my notion, too. Wish Jordan had let us pack a gun."

Sean composed himself in his bed, alert but not concerned. He caught flitting glimpses of the pair as they walked among the big beech trees. Both wore knee-length boots, red woolen coats, and had wool caps pulled over their ears. Little puffs of vapor trailed every breath they exhaled, for the day was very cold. Sean could not know that his nocturnal visits to Penny had been discovered, due to the fact he had left tracks in the snow.

As the men came nearer, Sean grew more anxious. Most times, when he did not move, men passed right by him. But this pair showed no sign of passing. Rather, they were exactly on his trail and coming straight to the thicket.

As they entered one side, Sean slipped out the other. Plainly there were times when he could escape detection by lying perfectly still and times when he could not. Snow seemed to have a bearing on whatever happened, and from now on he would have to watch himself in snow.

Sean slipped behind the trunk of a big beech tree and was careful to keep that behind him as he raced along. There was no outburst from the men who trailed him, nothing to indicate that he had been seen. The big Setter continued his effortless lope, anxious to put as much distance as possible between himself and the men who followed him. Only after an hour had passed, and the blowing wind brought no sign of anyone on his trail, did he slow to a trot.

From the top of a ridge he looked anxiously back. Nobody was coming, but Sean was worried. He sought another thicket and lay down, only to get out again when his trackers came within scenting distance.

This time Sean cut straight away, with no thought of stopping or of returning to Penny. He had been discovered and he must find safety. He traveled back toward Forks Valley. Night came again and still he trotted on.

Sean did not know that the men had followed him most of the day. Where he had jumped a snarling little creek they finally halted. They were satisfied. No pampered Irish Setter, they decided, would ever act in such a fashion. That night they trudged wearily back to Jordan Acres with the report that it was a wild dog that had come from the forest to visit Penny. The chances were that he would not come back. But, if he should come, they would be ready for him. Every night there would be wolf traps set in front of Penny's kennel run.

However, Sean had no intention of returning to the side of his new love in the immediate future. He had grown too wary and wise to make any foolish moves. It was best to stay away from Jordan Acres for at least a little while.

He crossed the head of Forks Valley and bristled at a scent that rose from the ground to his nose. Slasher had come back just as the snow stopped falling. His paw prints were plain in the snow, and it was to them that his cold odor clung. Sean sniffed interestedly. Slasher was heading south, toward the clearings.

The big Setter swung down to the creek where he had caught the suckers and unhesitatingly plunged into the ice-rimmed pool. Again the frightened fish swirled about him. Indifferent to the ice-cold spray that he raised, Sean galloped back and forth in the pool until he had caught another sucker. Emerging, he shook his heavy fur to dry it, and ate his fish.

He trotted up the creek's course, and stopped short

as he caught the scent of Tobe Miller's renegade heifer. His eyes sparking mischief, Sean stole toward her.

He found her in a little field beside the creek. Scraping snow with both front hooves, she was grazing on the frozen grass she uncovered. The heifer swung her head up as she caught Sean's odor and stood truculently, both feet braced. She grunted angrily.

Sean circled to one side and launched himself straight at her. The heifer spun on nimble feet to meet his charge and her horns raked viciously. But Sean was no longer there. Behind her, he was snapping gaily at her heels. Again the heifer whirled and again found nothing to fight. Sean was boring in from the side, nipping playfully at her flank. Finally the heifer backed to a boulder that jutted out of the slope and, her rear protected, stood ready to meet Sean should he come again.

But he was tired of the game. Keeping one wary eye on the heifer, he circled around her and continued his course up the creek's bed. Weary, he rested in the same copse of little pines from which he had started when his wandering steps had led him to Penny's side.

He stayed there until daylight had come again, then looked up into the pines to see the black squirrel practicing his endless leaps and bounds. Running up a limb to its slender tip, the black squirrel would launch himself into space just as the tip seemed ready to break beneath his small weight. Always he alighted on another limb and ran down it to jump again. Because he could not afford to take a chance, the black squirrel must teach himself over and over again every path in the pines. He knew the ones he could take and the paths nothing could leap. Now, should a winter-hungry marten pursue him to his chosen lair, the black squirrel had at least an even chance of getting away.

From off in the distance came three evenly spaced caws as Silverwing called his mate to a dead rabbit he had found. The cold would increase and the snow would deepen, but no matter how bitter the cold, or how deep the snow, the two ravens would survive because their two sharp brains always worked for the good of both.

Sean left the little pines and started back down the slope. He was hungry again, but he wanted no more fish if he could possibly get anything else. Fish was cold fare, but all right if eating was to be exclusively a matter of filling the belly. Red, hot meat was more to be desired.

A spring-born fawn ran out of his path, and for a little way Sean pursued it. He had never killed a deer, but he knew that venison was very good because he had eaten from Slasher's kill. The fawn outdistanced him and Sean turned his attention to other things. Not too far away he knew of several good thickets where rabbits played and ate, and thumped the earth with thudding hind feet when danger neared.

He crossed the very fresh trail of a hunting fox, and because the fox was traveling in the direction he wanted to go, he followed the trail for a ways.

Only a few minutes ahead of him, the fox entered the thicket Sean had in mind and criss-crossed it thoroughly. Sean sulked behind him. The fox had caught no rabbit, but he had frightened all of them into hiding. Sean followed him into the next thicket, and the one beyond that, and as he did he became more sulky. The fox did not lack enthusiasm, but evidently he was a young and inexperienced hunter. Though he caught nothing, neither did he neglect anything. No rabbit in any thicket had lacked attention, and in consequence there was not one left above ground. Nor would they come out of their burrows until they were sure the enemy had gone.

Disgusted, Sean left the fox's trail and struck off at right angles. He climbed the snow-covered slope on the other side of the creek, ran across its forested summit, and descended the opposite slope. Here was another region of thickets where rabbits abounded.

The big Setter first became aware of danger when a bullet from a high-powered rifle snicked into the snow scarcely five feet away. Then he heard the blast of the rifle.

His reaction was instantaneous. Dodging and twisting, he raced back up the slope he had just descended. The rifle cracked three times more, but no bullet landed near. The man on the other side of the valley was a hopeless distance away, and a racing target was ten times as difficult to hit as a stationary one.

Just before he broke over the crest of the hill, Sean heard the musical notes of a hunting horn. Almost at once the mournful bay of a trailing hound answered the summons.

Slasher had indeed returned to the clearings. Be-

cause he had not raided them in some time, the hill
men had been lulled into a false sense of security,
and Slasher had found wonderful hunting. Two
calves, half a dozen sheep, and five geese lay dead
behind him. Grimly resolved on full revenge, the
hill men and their hounds were out in force. But it
was not Slasher's trail the hounds were on; it was
Sean's!

He heard them reach the hill's crest where he had
crossed, and Sean stretched out to run. Only a greyhound can outrun an Irish Setter, and the yelling
pack was quickly left behind. Having never run in
front of hounds, unsure as to just what he should do,
Sean fell back to a trot.

Almost at once the hounds' swelling voices gathered volume and they drew near again. It was a
motley pack that pursued Sean. Everything from
cross-breeds to clean-limbed foxhounds were there.
Among the dogs were two that never touched a nose
to the ground, but just raced along. They were the
killers. When the quarry was finally cornered, their
job was to go in and pull it down. But also with the
hounds were two with long ears, quivering jowls,
and keen noses. No fighters, but trailers of vast experience, these two had never been known to leave the
scent of a quarry they started.

Again Sean lengthened out to run. This was something new in his experience, and he did not know
what to do about it. There was a coldly terrifying
quality in the steady voices of the pack. They could
not run as fast as he but they seemed to be tireless.
Their blended chorus was like the knell of death.

Sean circled into the wind, hearing the clamor of

the hounds but looking for men. The wind told him nothing, but he was sure the men were coming. Beyond much doubt they would come from the same direction as the dogs, so it was well not to go back there. Sean set a course that took him ever deeper into the wilderness.

The day wasted and evening came. Sean was bewildered now, and fatigued. He could still, in a little spurt of speed, draw so far ahead of the dogs that he could not even hear them. But it was impossible to lose them. Sean splashed through a stream, and waded out the other side. The pack did not even hesitate at the place he had crossed. The two experienced hounds with them were familiar with every trick that hunted creatures used.

Panting hard, hot in spite of the bitter wind, Sean paused a minute. The shifting winds had brought him the scent of Slasher, lying up in a thicket on the exact course Sean wanted to run.

The big Setter did not hesitate or change direction, for he was still unafraid of Slasher. He saw the coydog rise to challenge him, and Sean prepared himself for the uneven fight. Slasher was rested and comparatively fresh, while Sean had run, much of the time at full speed, for hours on end.

Head low, tail stiff, ruff bristled, Slasher waited for his enemy. Sean side-stepped and feinted. Then, very distant and faint, the mingled voices of the hound pack came to them.

Slasher was gone as silently as a breath of wind. So swift and so unnerving was his departure that Sean was left bewildered. One second Slasher was before him. An eye wink later only his scent remained to prove that he had ever been there. But he must waste no time wondering about Slasher. The hounds were coming fast. Sean raced down the rim of the hill.

The pursuing pack no longer ran as a unit. It had spread out, with the faster dogs ahead and the rest arranged according to their speed. Leading was a whippet-like youngster with a voice like a clear bell. Trailing him closely were the two killer dogs, who did not tongue at all. Rising steadily behind were the voices of the two experienced trailing hounds, who now ran near the center.

Coming to the place where Sean had met Slasher, the leading hounds broke into a sudden, half-hysterical yelling. Led by the trim hound with the bell-like voice, all but two of the dogs streamed off on Slasher's hot trail. Only the two older hounds, the pair that never left the trail until they found the game they wanted, remained on Sean's scent.

Night fell, and with its coming went all danger from men with rifles. Sean descended a wild little ridge, jumped the stream at its foot, climbed the slope on the opposite side, and rested in a grove of hemlocks. There he sat on his haunches and listened for the two hounds.

He heard them, all too soon, the relentless voices of pursuit. Whip-thin, tireless, the two old hounds did not know how to quit. Reluctantly, Sean ran on. Neither of the hounds was very fast, but both were steady, and they covered a lot of ground if given time. Again Sean was driven from his bed, and again.

Night faded, morning came, and still the voices of the two old hounds blended together in the deep wilderness behind him. Sean slowed to a trot, then to a walk. He had run as far as he intended to run. Panting up a boulder-studded hillock just as the sun broke over the horizon, he turned around to face the two hounds that were still on his trail.

When the first faint streak of dawn thinned the black mantle of night, Jake Busher got stiffly up from the fire beside which he and four others had spent the night. There had been some sleep, but not much, for every time all five men slept, the fire died and bitter cold awakened them. Jake blinked eyes that were reddened by lack of rest and by constantly straining into the north wind that had keened in his face all day yesterday. He ventured into the semi-darkness of early morning, kicked a dead stump loose from its frozen roots, and threw it onto the fire. Sparks flew, and the fire flared fitfully.

Like all the rest, Jake was tired and short-tempered. All day yesterday their hound pack, the best they could put into the field, had trailed and failed to overtake the red dog. Then the pack had split, with five hounds running after one dog or wolf and Joel Carter's prize pair running another. Following, hoping for a shot or a kill, the disappointed hunters had been night-bound in this cold valley.

As the rest of them woke up, Tobe Miller said surlily, "Got any bright ideas, Price? You was the one said he couldn't run away from us on a snow."

"Seems like I was wrong," young Price Allen admitted. "He did run away. All I can figure is to call the dogs in and try again."

"Them dogs can be halfway to Canada by now," Jake Busher grumbled. "We'll never find 'em."

Joel Carter said flatly, "I ain't goin' back 'thout mine are with me." He looked angrily at the fifth member of the party, his brother Vince. "How come you missed that red dog when you had four shots at him? If you could shoot straight, we'd be home now 'stead of roostin' in this Godforsaken valley."

"Ah, shut up!" Vince snarled.

Price Allen said, "Well, I aim to have a try at callin' 'em in."

He lifted the hunting horn that was suspended around his neck, warmed the mouthpiece with his fingers, and blew three clear, sweet notes on it. Nobody paid him the slightest attention. It had been a hard hunt and a miserable and hungry camp. All were too intent on their own physical distress to take interest in anything except building up the fire. An hour later the young hound that had led the pack limped into camp on three legs. He was one of the five that had followed Slasher, and finally brought him to bay. The young hound's left side and left front leg were ripped and scored by slashing teeth. Five minutes later, unwounded, two of the other hounds joined him. Of the five that had been on Slasher's trail, only these three would ever again respond to the call of the hunting horn. The two killers were already frozen where Slasher had left them with their throats ripped out.

The men sat silently around the fire, waiting for the rest of the hounds to come in.

Almost at the same time, on the high, wind-swept, boulder-strewn hillock, Sean braced himself to meet the two hounds. He saw them come out of the brush and disappear among the boulders, two rangy, black and tan hounds with their noses to the ground. At regular intervals their rolling bay floated forth to echo back from the distance. The two were within six feet of the embattled Sean before they glanced up and saw him.

The hounds stopped in bewilderment. They had done their part. At last they had bayed the quarry that they had trailed so far and so long. Now they did not know what else to do. It was not their fault if there were no killers present to take over. Besides, their quarry was not a fox or a bear, but a dog.

The two sat on their haunches, looking curiously at Sean. Bristling, he stalked them. The hounds growled, and just as hostilely came to meet Sean. They sniffed noses, but there was really no reason for a fight here. All the hounds knew how to do, and all they had cared to do, was find Sean. At first stiffly, then amiably, three tails began to wag.

Because they were all tired from the long chase, the three curled up so they could keep each other warm, and peacefully went to sleep.

7. Abduction

The noon sun shone coldly through a bank of gray clouds when the two hounds rose, stretched, wagged a friendly farewell, and started for Joel Carter's cabin. Sadly Sean watched them go. It had been nice to have friendly company, if only for a little while.

He sat on his haunches while the pair trotted slowly away. Again the aching loneliness flooded him, but he made no effort to go with the hounds. Though he liked both of them, he felt no strong attachment for either. Besides, their scents told him that they were Joel Carter's dogs and Joel was a stranger.

For a while Sean was plagued by memories of Billy Dash, Danny Pickett, Ross Pickett, and the life he had lived in the Pickett clearing. But all that was changed. No longer was he a pampered, prized dog but a wild thing to be hunted and shot at. There was nobody except himself to feed and take care of him, now.

He sat until the hounds went out of sight over the rim of the boulder-strewn knob, then got up, put his nose to their trail, and followed them a little way. But his hunger soon recalled him to the stern realities of wilderness life. For almost twenty-four hours he had run ahead of the hound pack with nothing to eat.

Sean started out to hunt. The wind, cutting steadily from the north, blew in his face and plastered his red fur close against his body. A few snowflakes whirled about him, clung to his fur for a moment, and dropped off. The sunny part of autumn was definitely gone, and the weather was turning bitterly cold as real winter set in.

Because rabbits were easiest to hunt, Sean went first to a likely looking thicket. He slunk into it, careful to make as little noise as possible while he sought a good ambush. His life in the woods had taught him to choose such places carefully.

A successful ambush was usually where he himself could be hidden or partially hidden by a clump of brush, a stump, a fallen log, or some other natural feature. At the same time, any ambush where he hoped to catch a rabbit must be heavily laden with rabbit odor, a signal that many rabbits ventured there. It was worse than useless to try to hunt anywhere else.

There was almost no rabbit scent. The thicket abounded in burrows but the bitter weather had driven their owners into them. Only occasionally did Sean find a place where a rabbit had ventured out to feed, and ducked back into a burrow as soon as it had eaten. It was no use.

Sean struck straight across the wilderness, back toward the creek where the suckers lived. Though fish were cold eating, certainly they were better than an empty belly. On the way he came to a wooded summit where straggling patches of laurel, rhododendron, and blackberry briers grew among the trees.

A puff of snow seemed to explode right in front of his face and something dashed away. Sean gave instant chase as the creature bounded behind a patch of laurel and stretched out to run.

This was not a cottontail rabbit but a snowshoe hare, and it was wearing a pure white coat that all snowshoes don when winter comes. Ravenous, Sean leaped clear over a patch of laurel and raced madly after the fleeing snowshoe. But the big-footed hare was nowhere to be seen.

Sean sniffed eagerly at other fresh tracks, which were all about. No matter how hard the wind blew, or how searing cold made tortured trees creak, the big snowshoes never sought shelter in burrows, but always stayed on top of the ground. Their safety lay in their white fur, an almost perfect camouflage against white snow, in their ability to twist and dodge, and in their sensitive ears. So keen was the snowshoes' hearing that they could detect the almost noiseless strike of a great horned owl.

Sean ran by sight, like a greyhound. It was not his nature to trail game, so he chased and lost another fleeting snowshoe that sped from him like a white spirit on the white snow. Hopefully he laid an ambush at a place where there was a heavy concentration of scent, but none of the big hares came along and Sean was too hungry to be patient long enough. He rose and prowled restlessly through the thicket.

There was a sudden, spitting snarl, and Sean halted abruptly. He had been so interested in snowshoe scent that he had paid no attention to anything else. Now he found himself face to face with a mottled lynx that had also come to the thicket to catch his dinner.

The lynx lay on a log overlooking a runway, and so wonderfully did his patched gray fur match his surroundings that Sean wasn't sure he saw anything at all until the lynx opened his mouth to spit again. With a happy yelp, Sean sprang to the attack.

The lynx leaped from his log and was running when he landed. Two jumps ahead of the insanely pursuing dog, the lynx leaped six feet up the trunk of a tree and clung there, snarling.

Without breaking stride, Sean launched himself into the air. His big jaws snapped shut, catching a fold of the lynx's skin as they did. Surprised because he had thought himself out of harm's way, the stung lynx scrambled farther up the tree. He looked down, spitting insults. After a minute the lynx climbed all the way up the tree, composed himself on a limb, and went to sleep.

Sean wasted ten minutes in senseless barking at the lynx and in rearing against the tree trunk. Finally he left to wander on. Chasing the big cat was fun, but now Sean was far too hungry to do anything except look for food.

He came to a wide meadow which, except for a cluster of wild apple trees in the center, grew almost entirely to long, tangled brush and short grass. Five deer, feeding on frozen apples they had scraped out of the snow, raised white tails over their backs and loped gracefully away as Sean approached.

The big Setter drooled as he snuffled hot deer scent. Since feeding from Slasher's kill he had hoped to have some more venison. But, though he had chased many deer, he had yet to catch one. He looked toward the deer; they had run only about forty yards and were impatiently waiting for him to get away from the apples.

Sean picked up a frozen apple and crunched it in his teeth. It was cold, filled to the core with ice crystals, but it was food. He ate half a dozen more apples and trotted on, his belly still empty but not as complaining as it had been.

Almost as soon as he left the trees the deer came back to fight over the remainder of the apples. Sean trotted across the snow-laden meadow, back into the forest, and came to a sudden halt as the stale scent of man wafted to his nostrils.

Cautiously he circled so that the strongest winds blew from the scent to him. The man had been here yesterday, but he was not here now. Besides, another scent almost drowned his. It was fresh, hot odor of a snowshoe.

Sean slunk forward, careful not to let himself be seen until he had looked around carefully. He edged out from behind a big beech tree and looked at a trail packed by a man on webbed snowshoes. About ten feet from the trail, a snowshoe hare, with a steel trap on both front paws, strained as far backward as the trap chain would let him go. Sean had struck the trap line of Crosby Marlett, who spent every winter season taking his furs in the wildest and most inaccessible places he could find.

Sure that there was no man around now, Sean padded across the trail to the trapped hare. Carefully he circled. Something, he did not quite know what, was amiss here. Though Sean wanted the big hare, he did not want to run into trouble getting it. However, he could neither see nor smell danger.

He leaped, struck, and the trapped hare quivered in his jaws. Sean wrenched it loose from the trap. Suddenly, the snowshoe still dangling from his jaws, he jumped as though he had come into unexpected contact with a hot electric wire.

Unknowingly he had brushed and sprung the second trap of the set. It clicked cold jaws against his paw and left a numbing sting there as it slid off without a firm grip. Sean hurried away. This was a new source of food but plainly it was not without its perils. From now on, he must be doubly careful and on the lookout for sudden surprises.

Sean ate the hare, then followed the trap line. He came across a trapped red fox that fluffed its fur, crouched low to the ground, and snarled at him. Curious about the fox, Sean stopped to look it over and trotted on. The big Setter would chase and if necessary kill a fox, but only desperate hunger could prod him into eating one.

As he went on, Sean found out more about traps. Coming to a trapped weasel that raged at him, Sean turned and contemptuously scratched frozen chunks of snow over the little animal. Its hair-trigger pan sprung by an ice lump, another trap clicked viciously into the air as its jaw closed on nothing. There was, then, a way to render traps harmless.

For three days Sean stayed on the trap line and fattened himself on trapped snowshoes. At the end of that time, Crosby Marlett ran his lines and Sean quietly faded away.

He was back in familiar territory now, and knew the best routes to go wherever he wished in that section of back country. Not necessarily the easiest ways, the paths he chose had plenty of cover and most of them led through game country where there was a good chance of getting food.

Sean pushed through a fringe of dwarf hemlocks and looked down upon a little stream that leaped between snowy banks. Some of the more sluggish waters were already frozen. Some, like the little stream before him, were so swift that they never froze completely and were only partially ice-locked in the coldest weather.

Where the stream split around a big boulder, Sean sprang from the bank to land squarely on that boulder. At once he gathered himself for the leap that carried him to the crest of the opposite bank. He disappeared into the hemlocks.

This was one of his regular crossings and he used it often. Always he employed the big boulder as a steppingstone. Not afraid of getting wet, he had no wish to wade or swim in frigid water when there was no need to do so. Sean struck through the hemlocks on a course that would bring him to the sucker-infested creek.

That night he slept again in the little pines. High in one of the bigger trees, the black squirrel rested snugly in a leafy nest of his own making. Silverwing and his mate, side by side, tucked their black heads under their black wings and slept while the night crackled with cold. Gaunt and cold, the renegade heifer stood with her back to the lashing wind and, in her own way, pondered the truth that freedom is a hard-bought thing. The heifer could have been warm, safe, and well-fed, in Tobe Miller's barn, but she preferred this wild life of her own choosing.

Dawn had not yet come when Sean left the little pines to set out in the darkness. Hunger, as usual was the force that drove him. Nor was Sean alone. From now until the spring sun shone warm again, hunger would be the specter that, awake or asleep, would haunt every creature that had to make its own way in the wilds.

Coming to the creek where he had fished so often, Sean found it sheathed in an impenetrable armor of ice. He sniffed hopefully but to no avail. There was no way that an animal as big as he could get beneath the ice, though the tracks of a hunting mink proved that he had found entrance through an air hole at one side of a pool. Sean shoved his muzzle deep into the hole and drank deeply of the mink's scent. He scraped the ice with both front paws.

A sudden squalling screech like that of an angered cat split the near-zero air. The mink had indeed dived into the air hole and tried to go under the ice, but he had found the slippery top surface anchored fast to the bottom. The pool was frozen all the way down and there were no fish that any hunter could get.

His brain on fire because he had failed, the mink hopped across the ice in short little jerks and flung himself at Sean. A tiny thing, weighing no more than a couple of pounds, even in his normal moments the mink was all bloodthirsty fury. Angered, he was a demon. He reached for and sank his teeth into Sean's cheek.

Sean whipped his head, flung his tiny tormentor into the air and caught him with strong jaws before he fell back to the ice. Sean's teeth ground through the mink, then he cast the limp body aside. Sean rather liked the powerful scent that the dying mink emitted from his musk glands, but the mink himself was as thin and tough as a rawhide whip. He would be poor fare on a night as cold as this.

Sean padded up the frozen creek, staying on the ice and snuffling both banks. His nose twitched, and, as though pulled by an invisible string, his head turned suddenly sidewise. A hundred yards up the slope, the same lynx that he had chased out of the rabbit patch had caught and killed a little raccoon. Sean bounded toward the cat.

Until he was within one bound, the lynx stood over its quarry and snarled, hoping to bluff the big dog. Then, as usual, the cat's nerve broke. It raced toward the nearest tree, sprang into it, and came down only when it discovered that there was no pursuit. The lynx stalked angrily away to hunt again.

Sean stood over the little raccoon, a yearling that should have been asleep in some secluded den. But this raccoon had wakened from its winter's sleep for one more hunt that had been its last. Sean gorged himself on fat, juicy flesh and retired to a thicket to sleep.

There was no thaw, no warmth, and the north wind blew almost steadily while the cold became more intense. Already, with the season not yet into its hardest stage, some deer lay frozen in their beds; the hurt or ailing had no chance. Given a touch of summer sun they might have survived. As it was, they died swiftly. Only the strongest and most cunning would be alive when spring came.

Sean remained strong and, as he ranged, his cunning grew. Born with the native intelligence of a dog, the necessity for just surviving had given him the craft of a wild thing. Thus, with no danger to himself, because he knew how to do it, he robbed Crosby Marlett's traps, took kills from the lynx, teased the renegade heifer, and lost only a little weight when many creatures that shared his wild range were gaunt with winter hunger.

But there was one blessing enjoyed by the black squirrel, the deer, the snowshoe rabbits, and even the mice, that Sean lacked completely. Although they might be hungry, they knew none of the heart-aches and the vain, wild yearnings that tortured the dog. They had been born to lead the lives they were living. Sean was tormented because he had not. He needed something that he did not have: companionship.

Thus, often when he was not hungry, he prowled the ridges and valleys in the hope that he would run across something to fulfill his greatest need. Secretly he followed Crosby Marlett when the trapper came to run his trap lines. Without going near the houses, he even prowled around Tobe Miller's and Jake Busher's farms. At the Carter place he became bold enough to sniff noses with the two big hounds that had slept with him on the rocky knob.

The answer lay in nothing he could find. Though he was able to take care of himself, Sean was not sufficient unto himself. He needed more than the wilderness could offer.

The sky was dark with heavy banks of clouds when, with an unswerving purpose, Sean started off one day across a mountaintop. Driven to desperation by the fact that there was nothing to share his life, he was setting off again for Jordan Acres.

Twenty minutes after he started, snow began to fall. It did not come as cottony fluff, but as hard, wind-driven pellets with almost the consistency of hail. The beech forest came alive as crisp snow rattled against the big trees' trunks and hissed down through the twigs. Here and there a twig or branch broke and fell. Ice-hard, wind-whipped snow stripped bark from some branches, leaving them scarred and naked.

Sean bent his head to the wind and padded onward. Underfoot, sand-like snow bunched in his paws, so that every now and then he had to stop and nibble out the miniature snowballs that clung to his ragged fetlocks and froze between his toes. He continued to trot on, and then was slowed to a walk by the storm's very fury. But not once did he flinch or turn aside. He had a definite destination in mind and nothing could swerve him from it.

Toward evening the bitter north wind died and for a little while there was a lull in the storm. With nightfall the wind shifted to the southwest. For the first time in days there were temperate breezes instead of frigid ones. The weather warmed to well above the freezing point, and still snow continued to fall.

It descended now in tumbling curtains that twisted and blew like ghost draperies as the winds tumbled them about. Falling on top of the near-sleet that already covered the ground, the snow heaped itself into feathery drifts and soft windrows. Had it been daylight, visibility would have been cut to ten yards and even that would have been blotted out when an especially powerful gust of wind whipped the snow about. It was the hardest fall of early winter.

Plowing through drifts as deep as his breast, going around when he could not go through, Sean continued to plod onward. He did not trot now; just to walk was exhausting labor. But he did not stop. Rabbits lay in their burrows, deer huddled together and let falling snow cover them, grouse gathered in thickets. In such a storm no animal except a dog with a purpose would have been abroad.

Finally exhausted from his battle with the storm, Sean halted on a beech-grown ridge. He scraped a hole in the snow, lay down in it, and let falling snow cover him while his own breath melted a hole through the covering. Sean slept the sleep of the utterly weary, paying attention to nothing and knowing that nothing would bother him.

In the morning he awakened, burst out of his hole, and shook clinging snow from his fur. He was fresh and rested, with no lingering stiffness and no sore muscles. Again Sean had proven his abundant vitality and health.

Hungry, he stumbled through the drifts, looking for a likely place to hunt. While he had slept, the weather had again changed. The wind, shifting back to the north, was now raw and biting. The temperature was dropping fast, and renewed cold froze a hard crust on the wet snow. But the crust was not yet hard enough to bear Sean's weight. At every step he broke through.

The big Setter stopped suddenly, snuffled about, and began to paw. Snow flew rapidly on both sides as he scraped vigorously with his front paws. A moment later he exposed the half-frozen flank of a dead buck that had been too old and feeble to survive the storm.

Carefully, remembering the strychnine-poisoned carcass of the doe, Sean ate his fill. He marked the place for future reference. By now he had been in the wilds long enough to know that hunting for a living was always uncertain. It would not come amiss in the future to know where there was an ample store of venison.

Though he had slept for hours, he curled up beside the dead buck and slept again. His was the inborn sense of a wild thing, that might have to move for days on end and that rests when it can. In addition, he had come here on a mission. He was wise enough to know that any hasty or ill-timed act on his part could not only defeat his purpose but might result in disaster. Not until night had fallen did he venture out of his bed.

The wind had died, but piercing, savage cold had clamped like a vise over the wilderness, and had made the snow's crust strong enough to bear Sean's weight. There was no moon, only an eerie half-light that peopled the forest with grotesque shadows. Frost rimed every trunk and glittered in the air. Cold-tortured trees snapped like rifle shots.

Paying no attention to the frost that clung to his whiskers, or to the fact that every breath congealed in a short little puff of cold mist, Sean raced happily along. It had been a long and hard journey, but he was nearing its end. Gone was his great sense of loneliness and his ache for companionship, for he knew that very soon he would have what he craved.

Yesterday it had been a struggle just to travel. Tonight, on the crusted snow, Sean flew along as effortlessly as he would have raced over a concrete highway. He broke out of the forest into the Jordan clearing and stood a moment to reconnoiter. From the tenant houses lights glowed through frosted windows. The big house was alight and the heavy smell of smoke from wood-burning fireplaces scented the night air.

Half-visible in the faint light, Sean trotted unhesitatingly toward the kennels. He made no attempt to slink or hide, for he knew that the night hid him anyway. Taut as a strung bow, he came to Penny's kennel run.

She slid out the kennel door, hesitant and nervous. Then she recognized him. A glad little whine of welcome escaped her and she flung herself forward to meet him. Sean stretched full length on the snow, and licked her extended cheek tenderly.

Beneath the crust on which he lay, three wolf traps were ready to seize his paws with toothed jaws. Sean was wholly unaware of their presence, and the traps were harmless anyway. Hidden beneath the hard crust, they might just as well have been under a layer of solid concrete.

Penny enticed him into a romp, and they raced back and forth across the kennel run. They reared, sniffing each other, and again lay side by side just so they could be close. Sean whimpered happily. Until now, he had lacked something as important as life itself. Now he had what he needed, and he was happy.

Penny leaped halfway up a long, sloping drift that lay in one corner of her kennel run and that reached nearly to the top of the wire fence. She sprang down again to land near Sean. He leaped beside her and they touched noses through the fence.

It was a delightful game. Again Penny leaped up the frozen drift, clawed in the slippery surface to get farther up, and jumped down. On the other side of the wire, Sean crouched in the snow like a puppy, front quarters spread and rear end elevated as he welcomed her. A half-dozen times Penny leaped at him while they played their own version of king-of-the-hill.

The night hours wasted all too swiftly, and Sean looked worriedly around when an early riser in one of the tenant cabins lifted a stove lid. There was a metallic thud as the lid was replaced, then the smell of fresh wood smoke rose on the air.

Sean backed reluctantly away, and was instantly recalled by Penny's anguished wail. He returned to sniff noses with her, and again looked anxiously at the tenant cabins. Not forgotten were the bitter lessons taught him by the hill men. He must not be caught here by anyone. Again he started away.

Penny's thin wail of protest floated into the winter darkness, and Sean returned to her once more. He stood with all four feet braced while he stared in amazement. For Penny's fertile brain had given birth to an idea.

There was no way to go through the wire, but there

might be a way over it. The crusted drift reached
two-thirds of the way to the top of the fence, and
Penny was halfway up the drift. She clawed furiously for a better foothold, almost fell off, then resumed her unsteady progress. Again she slipped,
lost all she had gained, and only stopped her downward descent by a previously clawed paw hold.

Slowly she resumed her climb. Very careful, main-
taining a slippery balance, she reached the top of the
fence, sprang from it and landed on all four feet at
Sean's side. They raced away on the snow's crust.

The early-rising tenant, looking through a hand-
warmed hole in a frosted windowpane, saw the two
dim figures in the morning's half light and decided
that they were two prowling foxes come to snoop
around the clearing.

8. Fugitives

Billy Dash's trip had been neither long nor dangerous. It had merely been monotonous. Traveling by night and lying up by day, he had never gone near a trail or road and he had met no one. Nor, of course, had he been seen by anyone.

Although Billy did not know it, the State Troopers had dropped their active search and placed his case in their files. Billy would not be forgotten, nor would the hunt for him ever be entirely dropped. Sometime and somewhere he would turn up. When he did, the ponderous machinery of the law would begin to grind and Billy would be brought back to face his punishment.

The specter of such a thing haunted Billy Dash day and night, but he did not allow it to dominate him. He had seen too much uncertain living to be unduly worried. The present mattered, and for the present he was free. He had better act accordingly.

Ever since he had left his own cabin, his goal had been an abandoned shack near an old coal mine. Before Billy was born, mining the vein of coal had proven so unprofitable that all working operations had been halted. Now trees four inches thick grew in the road down which teamsters had taken their coal. The place was so forsaken and so far back in the wilderness that almost nobody went near it, and few even remembered it. There was no timber here to attract a sawmill, no startling natural beauty that would bring sight-seers, and hunters did not have to come so far in order to find good hunting.

Five years ago, just rambling through the mountains, Billy Dash had come upon the place and had at the time fixed in his mind its natural advantages as a hideout should he ever find himself in need of one.

Coming back to it now, his first task was to fix it up. The walls were in disrepair, the roof leaked, and the interior had become the home of countless deer mice. Billy patched the roof with slabs of bark which he overlapped so that no rain could penetrate. From a nearby swamp he dug mud and mixed it with grass, and used this mixture to chink the cracks in the cabin's sides. Then he cleaned the place thoroughly, hauling water in a rusty dishpan he was lucky enough to find. He also discovered some odds and ends of dishes, and a little tableware. Billy scoured them with clean sand until they shone like polished steel.

The vermin problem was a hard one to solve until, suddenly, it solved itself. A curious brown weasel came down from the ridge to look through the open door and see what was going on. The weasel saw Billy Dash, working furiously with a broom which he had fashioned out of willow wands bound to a handle with some grapevine. When Billy turned around and saw him, the weasel dived beneath the cabin. There he found such excellent hunting that he saw no reason to leave.

Aware of the value of such a companion, Billy

never molested him. Within a week the weasel had overcome his fear of the man to such an extent that he did not hesitate to slip into the shack through a crack between two floor boards even while Billy was present. With tireless energy the weasel pursued the myriad deer mice to the farthest nooks and crannies. Watching him, Billy realized that before long both he and the weasel would be exhausting their food supplies in the cabin. That did not worry him unduly. They had both lived off the country before and they could do it again. If sometimes it was a poor or a monotonous living, that could not be helped.

Much more important was the fact that they had had no visitors. As winter advanced, there would be no likelihood of any. Nobody was going to hike sixteen miles through snow just to look at an abandoned coal mine and a tumbledown cabin. When spring returned a venturesome hiker might come, but Billy would worry about spring after it arrived.

For the next ten days Billy busied himself chopping a great store of firewood which he stacked on all sides of the cabin. He left the window unobstructed and enough space to swing the door open, but otherwise the cabin was banked to the roof with firewood. That would help keep the chinking in and the cold and storm out.

As he worked, Billy Dash pondered his future. He was a hunted fugitive, but his last consideration was walking in and giving himself up. It made no difference that the shooting of Uncle Hat was strictly accidental. It was enough that he was in trouble, and if he surrendered to the police, Billy thought, he would only be in more trouble.

With the first snow he stopped worrying about the possibility of being discovered, at least in the immediate future. But there were certain things that must be done. The meager supplies he had brought with him were almost gone; only scrapings and crumbs remained in the bottoms of the various cans and parcels.

Billy fingered the fifteen dollars pinned in an inner pocket. Somehow and some way he had to make contact with a store where he might get at least basic supplies, such as flour and salt. He himself dared not show his face near a store and he knew of no one who would act as his messenger. But Billy had an abiding faith that all problems could be worked out, and he was not yet desperate.

When the snowshoe hares donned white winter coats, a signal that fur was prime, Billy started out with his traps. He did not hope to catch a great store of fur and he hadn't the least idea of where he would sell it if he caught any. But the cabin was in good shape, he had plenty of firewood, and he was restless. He must have action of some sort because a man who had nothing to do was apt to start thinking too much about himself and his problems, and that was never good.

Billy made his first set under a cut bank where, as he saw by their tracks, mink had been running. The rest of the traps in his pack sack, he struck into the thickets where foxes would certainly be hunting.

This was primarily a scouting trip, meant to refresh himself on the lay of the land. Billy set no more traps for hours, and at noon sat down to lunch on a chunk of unsalted venison. Habit, more than the thought that someone might see him, made him seek the seclusion of a laurel thicket while he ate lunch, and it was natural for him to find a high knob from which he could see the surrounding country.

Billy was half through his lunch when he saw a man coming. He stiffened, let his hand drop to the big .45 at his belt. He took his hand away again. There must be no more shooting. It was far better simply to fade into the brush and avoid a meeting.

Billy was about to slip through the laurel when he recognized the approaching man. It was Crosby Marlett, the trapper. A hill man himself, Crosby was noted throughout the Wintapi as an expert trapper and a great man to mind his own business. Crosby Marlett was perfectly happy as long as he was left alone to do his trapping, and as long as nobody interfered with his traps, he was friendly.

Billy knew that the time had come to take a chance. He sat perfectly still until the trapper was opposite him, then spoke quietly.

"Hello, Crosby."

"Uh—Hello."

Billy rose. Crosby Marlett saw him, nodded, and amended his greeting.

"Hello, Billy. How you doin'?"

"Good enough. How 'bout you?"

"All right. I'm layin' out a new fox line."

"How fa' you goin'?"

"Allerton Crick."

Billy Dash said, "I'll stop at the Crick, then."

Crosby Marlett nodded. It was an entirely satisfactory agreement. They had divided the trapping territory, and each knew that the other would not trespass. Crosby looked at Billy's traps.

"Didn't know you was in this country, Billy."

"I get around."

"So I see." Marlett grinned at him. "You get far enough?"

Billy grinned back. "Well, I haven't got to the stoah at Cedar Run yet."

"I get there. Goin' next week."

"Then maybe you'd bring me some salt and flour and such-like?"

"Sure."

Billy Dash took a thin sheaf of bills from his inner pocket. "Spend it all," he said.

Crosby's adam's apple bobbed. "Maybe we should have a rondy-voo?"

"The big pine with the bent top at Allerton Crick would suit me."

"Me, too."

They parted, and Billy strode serenely homeward. He had made the necessary contact. Crosby Marlett knew very well that he was on the dodge; any man who was not could go to the store at Cedar Run for himself. But Crosby had not asked why, nor would he ask.

Four days later, when Billy visited the big pine with the twisted top at Allerton Creek, he found a packed parcel hanging in it. He took it without bothering to see what it contained. Crosby Marlett, who spent all his time in the woods, would know what other men doing the same thing should have.

As winter advanced, sometimes they met at the big

tree. More often Billy simply left his pack sack safely cached in one of the branches, with a few pelts in the sack. They were as good as money and the store-keeper at Cedar Run would take them in trade. No-body would think it unusual because Crosby Marlett was catching a large amount of fur, or that he needed an extraordinary amount of supplies. Besides, even if they might wonder, Crosby did not take kindly to questions about his personal affairs.

As soon as he and Penny reached the edge of the Jordan clearing, Sean stopped to look back. It was a gesture that his various skirmishes with men had taught him; he wanted to see his back trail and find out whether or not they were being pursued.

There was no sign of any life save the one faint light in the early-rising tenant's house. A door slammed as the tenant went from his house to the cow barn. Barn windows glowed when he snapped the lights on there. Satisfied, Sean turned to Penny.

She danced coquettishly away from him, her jaws spread in a doggy grin, then whirled and ran. Sean made no attempt to interfere because she was run-ning into the forest and not back to the clearing. He had won. He had a companion to travel with him and now he did not care where they went as long as they stayed away from any place where people lived.

Deliberately holding himself back so that his head was even with her shoulders, Sean ran with Penny. He could outdistance her if he wanted to, but it was enough just to have her with him and to know that there would be no more lonely days and nights. She whirled, and without breaking stride, took a playful nip at his ear. In the same motion she dodged away, then dived purposefully in to strike his shoulder with hers.

She struck hard enough to knock him sideways. Sean clawed for a hold on the glazed crust, recovered his balance, and closed his big jaws over her front leg when she followed up the attack. Like a pair of overgrown puppies they frolicked and leaped. They reared, front paws clawing at front paws and heads diving and ducking for a hold. Neither had, and neither wanted, the advantage. This was strictly play, a wonderful frolic such as Sean had not enjoyed since leaving Danny Pickett's clearing.

Running beside her, playing when she felt like playing, Sean guided them deeper into the beech woods. Without knowing why he did it, she followed willingly when he circled to get into the wind.

Sean analyzed the air currents that blew in his nose and realized that they were not being followed. His restlessness departed. Nevertheless, now that his mission had succeeded far better than he had hoped, he wanted to put as much distance as possible between them and the Jordan place. They would be safe only in the deep wilderness that reached from the head of Forks Valley to the pines where the black squirrel and the ravens lived.

As dawn broke slowly out of a cloudy sky, they stopped to drink from a bubbling little stream and pushed on. Penny, going into the wilderness for the first time, had an overwhelming curiosity about everything around them.

She dashed at a red squirrel that had just finished his morning visit to a cache of beechnuts and was now returning to his nest in a hollow tree. Sean watched her indulgently, knowing that she wouldn't catch the squirrel but willing to let her have her way. Then she investigated a Canada jay that tilted on a branch, ran in mad pursuit of a covey of grouse that thundered up in front of them, and barked at a woodpecker that drummed high on the skeleton of a dead tree. She raced, barking hysterically, after a herd of deer that speedily left her behind.

Finally she licked hungry lips and sniffed expectantly about. Kenneled, Penny had received only one meal a day, but in the kennel she had needed no more. Since running away with Sean she had exercised more than she normally would in a whole week, and she wanted something to eat.

Sean watched her quizzically as she tasted a bit of snow, licked her lips again, and trotted toward a beech tree. Penny sniffed its trunk. She found nothing to eat there and no promise of anything, so when Sean came near she nipped him savagely. He backed off a few feet, unwilling to meet her punishing teeth with his own. When he started off through the beeches she followed sulkily along.

Sean had found the Jordan clearing only by accident, and he had stayed and returned only because Penny was there. But he had hunted close to it often enough so that he knew where some good hunting lay. He led Penny to a thicket where, as he remembered, a number of rabbits lived. As they entered the brush, Sean's nose told him that rabbits were feeding.

Driven underground by the first cold spell, the cottontails couldn't stay there any more than the grouse could huddle perpetually beneath the ever-greens or the deer could forever remain in warm shelters. All had to feed some time, and when the pangs of hunger became intense, all had to venture out.

Sean chose his ambush carefully, and slunk along toward it. Because this was a new and delightful game, Penny was willing to follow in his paw prints. Sean crawled behind a moss-grown stump that was surrounded by a few sprigs of laurel and blackberry canes. Here four trails crossed where cottontails came from four different directions to get to various feeding grounds.

Sean lay motionless, flat on the ground. His muscles were tense, ready to launch his body at the right moment. He smelled a cottontail coming and a second later he saw it.

In no hurry to rush into trouble, the rabbit was hopping along one of the four paths. The little brown beast halted beneath an overhanging arch of black-berry canes. The rabbit could be seen and it was well aware of that fact. Wise in wilderness lore, it had halted beneath the blackberries to see if it could tempt the strike of any predator that might be hunt-ing. Nothing happened. The rabbit continued its deliberate way, straight toward Sean's waiting jaws.

Suddenly, no longer able to contain the excite-ment that had trembled within her since her first sight of the rabbit, Penny leaped up and over Sean. Straight at the rabbit she dove. Never hesitating, the rabbit whirled, whisked its tail in Penny's face, and was gone. Penny gave near-hysterical chase.

Sean rose, knowing that his ambush was spoiled,

but holding no resentment because of it. Many of his ambushes had been ruined before. He prowled through the thicket, jumped at a rabbit that dodged away from him, then heard the unmistakable snap of Penny's jaws.

The rabbit she had chased had fled straight to a burrow and dived in. Penny was lingering at the burrow's mouth, drinking in the hot scent of the game she had missed, when Sean flushed the second rabbit. It had headed for the same burrow, completely unaware of Penny's presence. She twisted herself almost double to catch it, but she caught it.

When Sean came up to her, the limp rabbit dangled from Penny's jaws. She looked at Sean, growled a warning for him to keep off, and trotted away.

Penny laid her catch on the snow and pawed it with her foot. Accustomed to the food the kennel men gave her, she did not know quite what to do with this. If she had been well-fed she would have left the rabbit where it was. But she was hungry. Penny took an experimental bite, shook her head to clear her teeth of the fur and fluff that tangled in them, then was down to raw flesh. While Sean looked on, she ate.

Sean whirled suddenly to face the breeze. His head went up and his nostrils worked as he read the message it brought him. He looked questioningly at Penny.

Penny's abduction had finally been discovered and there were men coming. They came slowly for, in spite of the snow, the hard crust left no clear line of tracks. There were only scattered claw marks on the snow, and long stretches where there was not even that much. The pursuers could travel swiftly only when they came across a rare place where wind had whipped powdered snow across the crust and Penny and Sean had walked in it.

Penny, who had eaten everything except the rabbit's skin and paws, looked indifferently up when Sean warned her. Her sense of smell was as keen as his, and she, too, knew the men were coming. But Penny saw no reason for flight because she was acquainted with the men. None of them had ever hurt her.

Sean trotted into the brush, away from pursuit, and looked anxiously back. Puzzled, Penny followed him. But Penny was too new to the woods to understand what Sean wanted and she was not at all averse to welcoming the pursuers. She sat down on the crust and lifted a cold forefoot.

There was no hesitation and no uncertainty about Sean now. He bounded back to her side, and gone was all pretense of playing when he nipped her. Penny cried out, whirled to face him with bared fangs, then quailed before the sheer savagery of Sean's onslaught. Her ears flattened, her tail drooped. The next time Sean started away, she followed. She need not share the game she caught, but Sean was obviously going to make the decisions about when and where they should go.

He took her across forested ridges, down into the valleys that separated them, and up the opposite slopes. Not forgotten was the first lesson he had learned on snow; when the earth was snow-laden he could be followed. Though he had eaten nothing since feasting from the dead buck, Sean dared not stop to hunt.

The big Setter was guided by an inborn sense that is present in many animals and in some people. A hound-pressed fox will not go near its den, and thus betray its cubs. Billy Dash, in trouble, had not run to his home. Now Sean, pursued, did not take. Penny back to Forks Valley as he would have done had there been no men following them.

Sean led Penny southeast, on a course that led directly away from the wild valley. He had never been in this section before and knew nothing about it, but it was wilderness and that was all he wanted.

Penny limped on three legs now, the ball of her left front paw sore and bleeding a little from unaccustomed contact with rough snow. She swung in behind Sean and followed tiredly. When they reached a laurel thicket, she coaxed him into stopping. Side by side they lay, Sean's head over Penny's back as he kept his nose into the prevailing winds. An hour and a half after they stopped to rest, he caught the scent of the persistent trackers on their trail. Rested, Penny followed more willingly when Sean insisted that they strike off again.

They came to an unfrozen stream and Sean swung to follow its brawling course. A half mile down, a succession of quiet pools were frozen solid, and Sean led Penny out on them. Water had banked against the ice, flowed over it, and melted the snow. The glare ice was not so hard on Penny's feet as was the hard crust, and it was on the ice that Sean finally found something to eat.

A magnificent brown trout, fully two feet long, had come downstream with the rushing water, been washed over the ice with it, and now lay on its side, frozen solid. Sean's jaws had rended frozen food before and they could again. He ate his fill while the dainty Penny looked on disinterestedly. This was no proper food for a patrician Irish Setter.

Again they lay up in a thicket and again were routed by the pursuing men. Sean cut through a forest of gloomy, big pines, broke from them into slender aspens, and circled a little. Never was his circling or changing course without purpose; he always wanted to be where the winds blew to best advantage. They would tell him everything he wanted to know.

With night a full moon tilted on the crest of the tallest mountain, and by its light Sean and Penny traveled on. The moon waned, and utter blackness shrouded the wilderness. Until nearly morning the two lay up in a thicket, and morning brought a gently blowing west wind with more snow. Their tracks were hidden.

All that day Sean traveled slowly, and by nightfall was satisfied that the pursuers were no longer on their trail. At last, he could lead his new mate to the country he liked best. He struck an angling course that would take them back to Forks Valley.

Sean could not know that, in leading the trackers away from Forks Valley instead of toward it, he had thrown off pursuit for good. Penny was a valuable dog, a sure winner in any show, and the search would be continued. But it would center around here instead of in Sean's home range.

9. Frozen Hunger

Now that they had shaken all pursuit from their trail, Sean was no longer in a hurry. He loafed along, hunting when they were hungry, and resting when they were tired. Penny, very much the tenderfoot, never strayed very far from his side. Not only was she afraid to be alone, but she was learning to trust him. However, even though all this was new to her, and Penny lacked both the patience and the technique to lay a good ambush, she did have her own ways of hunting. They were unusual, but they worked.

Penny's first experience in a rabbit thicket remained firmly implanted in her mind. Paying no attention whatever to Sean, she sought the first burrow from which hot rabbit scent came in sufficient quantity, and stayed there. Sean, rambling around, was sure to flush a rabbit to her and Penny was quick enough to catch whatever came.

For a time Sean suffered poor hunting and scant rations. But he learned from Penny. When she caught a rabbit she always ate it and then she wanted to rest for an hour or more. But after she rested she overflowed with the surging energy and lively curiosity of a healthy Irish Setter. Fresh rabbit tracks were very intriguing. If Sean was patient with her, and let her eat and rest, and then led her to another thicket, Penny bounded all over it and left not the least sprig of brush uninvestigated. Sean, waiting at any promising burrow, was able to catch his own dinner the same way she had.

Side by side they traveled slowly on. Ten days after he stole her away from her kennel, Sean led Penny to his favorite bed in the little pines.

Silverwing, who had been out hunting, soared gracefully into one of the big pines, sought the lee side where the seething wind did not cut so fiercely, and alighted on a branch. His sharp eyes spied Penny and he chuckled hoarsely, calling his mate. When she came, the pair of them balanced on a swaying pine branch while they studied thoroughly this newcomer to their domain.

Penny looked up and barked at them. The pair of ravens, knowing perfectly well that they were out of harm's way, chuckled and cackled to each other. With precise aim, Silverwing dropped a pine cone on Penny's head. Penny merely nosed the cone as it rolled in the snow. The birds clucked in disappointment and flew off to see if they could find and bother the black squirrel. But the squirrel, who had no liking for winter and who ventured out of one of his several nests only to visit a cache of food, was curled up asleep.

The air seemed to crackle with frost, and when night reached its blackest point, Northern Lights flickered lonesomely in the sky. Bears lay in their hidden dens, raccoons nestled in hollow stubs, woodchucks were deep underground, and even the sun seemed to sleep most of the time behind a blanket of fleecy clouds. Almost it seemed that the creatures who had to stay abroad were cursed by nature. They were all hungry and getting hungrier.

Down over the rim, the black and white heifer pawed hopefully in the snow, and time after time went over ground from which she had already eaten the last shred of browse. When Sean and Penny came in, the heifer drifted out, and moved farther down the ridge in search of a new food supply.

Sean and Penny could not escape the Frozen Hunger, but compared to some they were in a fortunate position. In their search for food, they could at least move about freely. Rabbits, that had shivered in brush patches since rabbits were created, dared not venture too far away from them because they would be killed swiftly if they did. Deer huddled in their yards unless driven out by extreme hunger. Many deer, seeking more food, died in deep snow two days after they left packed yards. Even foxes were not as adaptable as the dogs. Foxes knew certain hunting places, and when game played out in a familiar area they were as apt as not to waste their energy on fruitless and desperate hunts rather than to seek better country.

Sean knew no such restrictions. He and Penny were the only two of their kind that ran wild, and as such they needn't fear trespassing on another's hunting grounds. And Sean, like most Irish Setters, was perfectly capable of fitting the act to the need. He would go anywhere, try anything, and he feared nothing.

Snowflakes dappled the air as he led Penny across the same meadow in which he had chased the deer herd away from frozen apples. Sean pawed hopefully beneath the trees, but the apples were long since gone and the deer had descended into a sheltered white cedar swamp to join others of their kind. The mass of deer together kept trails beaten so there was no foundering in snow, but their very numbers defeated their purpose. Only the biggest and strongest, rearing on their hind legs, could now get a full meal from overbrowsed cedar. The rest took what they could get, and starved if it was not enough.

Sean left the apple trees and continued across the meadow into beech woods. New snow lay on top of the old crust, so that they left a well-marked trail behind them. The snow was pellet-like, icy stuff, and the snapping cold bore no promise of any early thaw.

Again the rabbits were underground. They had been out earlier to snatch a few hasty mouthfuls of frozen grass or twigs, but they were not out now. Nor would they be until the weather softened a bit. Rabbit hunting was always at its best right after the weather broke and the sun shone for a while. This was not such a time.

Sean and Penny trotted on to hunt snowshoes across a timbered ridge. But the big snowshoes were hard to catch and overwary of ambushes. All day long the two tried, and failed.

Hunger pinched their bellies and cramped their throats. In this artic weather a lot of food was needed just to maintain body heat, and neither had eaten in almost eighteen hours. Then it had been a skimpy meal of a grouse they had found frozen in the snow.

Three miles away, Slasher, who had not been on Sean's range since the hound pack chased him, was enjoying rich living in the deer yard. But Sean and

Penny did not know about that. They had not stumbled across any deer yard.

There was a flutter of wings in a tree over them. Sean halted where he was, one forepaw lifted and his body tense. But the winging bird was only a blue jay that had come to rest in one of the giant beeches. Seeing the two dogs beneath him, hoping to stir up a fuss, the jay squawked a couple of times. He ruffled indignant feathers when Sean and Penny went on without paying any attention to him.

A pale moon glowed through shredded clouds when Sean finally led Penny back into the meadow. There was no evidence of any living thing except themselves. Not even a fox was there to hunt for mice beneath snow-arched tunnels. Sean swung into the broken path that he and Penny had trod earlier.

Without being aware of what had hit him, Sean stumbled forward in the snow so hard that his chin plowed a little furrow. He had been struck a tremendous blow on the spine, and hot little spasms of pain darted along his back. As he recovered, he saw Penny sprawl beside him. Sean whirled, his fangs bared and his ruff bristled.

The air was filled with floating shadows as noiseless as the vapor puffs that floated from Sean's mouth. Even as he turned, another of the shadows dived in to strike.

Sean struck back, leaping in and slashing at the same second. The shadow drifted away. Sean worked his lips to dislodge the feathers that clung to his teeth and lips, and leaped to Penny's side just in time to take upon himself a blow meant for her.

Dimly outlined against the wan moon, a dozen or

more great horned owls wheeled over the meadow. Weirdly silent, their flight made no tell-tale noise whatever. Ordinarily the owls, peerless hunters, flew alone and contented themselves with hares, mice, and small birds. But now, famished, and driven by starvation, this wolf-flight of owls was attacking the two dogs.

His muscles tense, ready in a split second to launch himself, Sean awaited the next attack.

Like a night shadow, and no creature of flesh and blood, one of the owls detached itself from the ghostly flight and descended to strike. Sean met it head on. His great jaws filled with fluffy feathers and sank through them into flesh. The owl snapped its beak in a chip-chop cadence, and powerful wings beat Sean's head and jaws. Sharp talons sank like hot irons into both his cheeks.

Sean relaxed his hold, surged forward, and bit deeper. He dragged the owl down onto the snow, clenched his jaws, and the owl's talons relaxed. The powerful wings spread out on the snow, and then the only sign of life was fluttering wing tips twitching feebly through shimmering layers of frost.

Locked in mortal combat with another of the raiders, Penny rolled over and over on the snow. Sean leaped again, fastened his teeth in an owl's thigh, and dragged it down. He held it with his paws while he unclenched his jaws to bite through its head. Sean saw Penny get up, leave the owl she had killed, and turn to face the others.

An owl dived squarely between them. Penny and Sean sprang from opposite sides. Each seized a wing and dragged the big bird down on the snow.

The rest departed on noiseless wings. In less than three seconds the only indication that the meadow had recently been a scene of savage strife were four dead owls on the snow.

Sean nosed one, tumbled it with his paws, and pulled out a mouthful of feathers. He bit deeply into stringy flesh and through small bones, and swallowed whole what he tore loose. The big Setter ate all except the legs and bill, left feathers tumbled on the snow, and then ate a second owl. Only when he had finished did he think to lick his wounded jowls with a soothing tongue.

Penny, working on the second of the two remaining owls, finished it a moment later. She nosed about for any stray bit that she might have missed, licked satisfied chops, and came over to caress Sean with her muzzle.

They trotted as far as the forest and lay down on the sheltered side of a big beech trunk. Tomorrow would bring its own problems, but tonight they had eaten.

Their only business was hunting, and if they did not hunt they could not stay alive. Always they were hard-pressed and usually their bellies were pinched. But they did eat and in their snowy beds they kept each other warm while the winter wore on. It was when snow lay deepest, and the situation was most desperate, that they had their biggest windfall.

As usual when they left a bed, they were hungry. Haunting rabbit thickets, trying unsuccessfully to catch or ambush snowshoes, their bodies were crying for food when Sean struck purposefully off across the snow. Suddenly he raced forward.

A beech forest lay ahead. In the trees, snow

heaped over her back, stood a doe so old that her head was white with age.

The doe had left a deer yard three days before. It was a rich and sheltered yard, where no deer died of starvation and few fell to predators. Yet, with plenty of food around her, fat in spite of the winter, the old doe had still chosen to strike out through the drifts. Spring was still a long way off, and this year its warmth would hold no promise for the old doe. She was that rare wilderness creature, one who has lived a full life and must die from old age. She had left the yard because some prompting within herself had bade her, in her last extremity, to die near this beech forest where she had been born and had taken her first wobbling steps.

She made no attempt to run or fight back when Sean and Penny swept upon her. The old doe was wise in the ways of the wilderness and its law. She knew when she left the yard that this, or something like it, must be her end anyway, and she did not care.

For a full week Sean and Penny ate well, until nothing but the old doe's bones were left to mark the place where, long ago, she had begun her life's journey. Then hunger, a seldom-absent companion, was with them again.

On a sparkling, frost-filled night when a full moon showed its round fatness to the snow-locked forest, Sean raced beside Penny as they crossed a frozen meadow on their nightly hunt. When a shadow exploded in front of him, Sean leaped full at it.

He missed, and cast cautiously about. A flock of grouse that by day filled themselves with buds from the nearby trees, by night had left the trees to plummet into the snow. As they struck, the impact of each body made a hole that became a warm bed.

The grouse were no fools. In spite of the fact that it was night, when grouse should be sleeping, the scrape and rattle of the racing dogs' paws alerted them. Each grouse lay in its bed, ready to burst into flight when the dogs came too near.

Sean was ready for the next one. He timed his leap perfectly, and when he descended a grouse fluttered in his jaws. Sean left the bird where it lay and leaped for another. He caught it, looked around, and trotted back to Penny.

Dragging by one wing the first grouse he had caught, she was investigating a wind-felled tree that had brought down more trees with it. Snow had arched the heaping trunks so that they formed a sort of cave.

When Sean came near, Penny snarled at him.

10. Wolf Trap

As winter wore on, Billy Dash tended his traps, picked up his supplies where Crosby Marlett had left them in the twisted pine, and tried not to think about the future. Early one morning, carrying enough furs to pay for a new load of supplies, he started for the pine at Allerton Creek. Crosby was already there, sitting beside a small fire he had built and blowing short, angry puffs out of a blackened pipe. The trapper glanced at Billy.

"Hi."

"Hi," Billy answered. Something was wrong, and if he waited long enough he might find out what it was. On the other hand, he might not. It was never a good idea to ask Crosby questions. The trapper took the pipe out of his mouth and held it in his hand.

"I'll get him this time!"

"That so?" Billy murmured politely.

"Yeah. He hit my trap line for a while last fall and then left it. Now he's back."

Billy's interest quickened. Crosby Marlett's private affairs were his own, but a trap-line pirate could easily concern both of them. Furthermore, Billy didn't like the idea of another visitor in these parts.

"Who is he?"

" 'Tain't a he," Crosby snorted. "It's a *it*. Wolf, I

reckon. Pirated my trap line last fall and spoilt I don't know how many sets! Now it's back!"

"A trap-robbin' wolf?"

"That's it."

"Nevah heah tell of such a thing."

"Nor did I, until now. Come on: I'll show you. The critter crossed the trail no more'n a hundred yards up."

Billy followed him, and squinted at the trail in the snow. He got down on his hands and knees to examine it. Wolf tracks and dog tracks were almost exactly alike, but there were minute differences that were sometimes revealed when the tracks were plain. Besides, wolves usually stayed as far as possible from anything that even looked like a trap. Billy furrowed his brows and looked up at Crosby Marlett.

"You shuah that's a wolf?"

"What else?"

"Dog."

"Well, dog or wolf, I aim to get him. He leaves the line to cross on that big rock down Fordyce Crick. Next time Mr. Trap Robber puts his paws on that rock, he's goin' to put 'em right smack in a wolf trap."

Billy nodded. "I know wheah the rock is: by a thick stand of hemlocks."

Crosby adjusted his pack. "Can't stand gabbin', Billy. Got to look at more sets, then I'm goin' down Fordyce Crick and set me a wolf trap. Want to come along?"

"No, thanks," Billy said.

Crosby disappeared. His brow still creased, Billy Dash watched him go.

Sean, carrying in his mouth a snowshoe hare that he had stolen from one of Crosby Marlett's traps, leaped over a snow-covered log, balanced lightly on the other side, and raced away. His course took him across a fire-scorched area that was almost devoid of trees and brush. Knowing very well that he was entirely visible as long as he remained in the burned place, Sean ran across it as fast as he could.

He ducked into some laurel on the other side of the burn and slowed his run to a fast trot. He was in a great hurry, but not so hurried that he could afford to overlook anything that might be on his back trail. Reaching the top of a hillock, the big Setter sought a place where he was well-screened by brush, and stopped. He sat down, the hare's dangling legs almost brushing the ground on either side of his jaws, and surveyed his back trail.

Finally, satisfied that he was not being followed, Sean trotted into a valley, stepped into a racing little rill that bubbled down it, and walked in the water for a hundred yards. He leaped out on the same side he had entered, and landed on all four feet in the center of a laurel patch. He slunk through the brush, crouching, and emerged from the laurel onto a razor-backed ridge. During the winter Sean had learned a lot about trails, and how to hide his own, and he put all his knowledge to use.

Six days ago, for the first time since winter had set in, the south wind had blown and the temperature had risen to spring-like heights. Much of the snow had melted, and for a while every little ditch and streamlet had fairly burst its banks with an excess of snow water. The bigger streams and creeks had become snarling torrents that rushed over the ice and would have melted it had not a sudden cold snap set in and frozen everything again.

The razor-backed ridge was bare of snow save for a few shady spots here and there, and Sean avoided those as he trotted on. When he came to the end of the ridge, he leaped to a boulder, climbed to another one, and looked down on his favorite grove of pines. Almost in their center was a nest of boulders, across which a great pine had fallen so that its massive trunk overthrust one end. Pine needles and forest litter had blown against both sides to form a cave that kept out much snow and cold.

It was there that Penny lay. Yesterday morning she had sat down beneath the pine's overhanging trunk and refused to move. When Sean had tried to coax her into a frolic, she had set upon him with lifted lips and punishing teeth. Penny had busied herself carrying some sticks and litter out of the cave and more back in. For three hours she worked, arranging the cave to suit herself. Nor had she allowed Sean to come near. A hundred feet from the cave marked a deadline beyond which she would not let him approach, for this was now sacred territory.

All day long Penny had stayed in the cave, suffering her own ordeal. The night had been half wasted when Sean finally set out to do her hunting for her. It was the way of the fox and the wolf, both of which respect and aid their mates in time of stress, and Sean was close enough to both so that he could make it his way.

Now, very respectfully and very slowly he started

toward the cave. Reaching the deadline, he was warned by Penny's fierce snarl. Sean dropped the big hare and beat a hasty retreat.

At a safe distance he sat down, paws braced and tail straight behind him. He pricked up his ears and lolled his tongue as he heard a faint series of squeaks and mewlings, not unlike those of young kittens. Interested as he was, he knew it was not for him to come any nearer at the present time. Penny would decide the proper moment for him to become acquainted with the nine pups that she nursed beneath the fallen pine.

Sean lay down and rested his head on his paws. He saw Penny appear at the end of the pine's trunk. She hesitated there a long while. Only five feet from the pups, she was terribly worried about them. Before she went farther away, she wanted to be sure that nothing able to harm them lurked within striking distance. Satisfied that there was nothing dangerous present, Penny raced to the snowshoe Sean had left, snatched it up, and immediately ran back to the cave.

She disappeared within. The puppies, whose mewling had grown loud when Penny left them, quieted when she came back. Only an occasional squeak mingled with the sound of the soft breeze that set the pine branches to whispering among themselves.

The black squirrel, indifferent to the dogs as long as they did not molest him, practiced his jumping and leaping through the pines. Silverwing, who knew very well that something strange had invaded the pine grove, tilted on a swinging branch and cocked his head to listen. He had never heard anything like this before and he couldn't figure it out. Finally he flew away to find his mate. When the ravens returned to the pine grove they rested in the outer fringe of trees and did not go near the cave.

After half an hour Sean rose to trot away. He had brought something for Penny to eat, but he had eaten nothing himself and was very hungry. He trotted swiftly through the pines, following the same path he had used when he came in.

Had Sean been in a kennel he might have given the puppies no thought. But he was not in a kennel, and running wild had sharpened his wild instincts. It seemed perfectly logical for Penny to stay with, nurse, and protect the puppies while he did the hunting for both of them. The puppies could not possibly feed or defend themselves. Later, when they were big enough, the natural course of events would be for both Sean and Penny to take them out and teach them how to hunt.

Safely away from the pines, Sean broke into a fast run. Often when he and Penny had hunted together they had gone hungry. Now that he had to find food for both of them his responsibility was tremendous. But Sean knew where there was always food to be had. Although he had purposely kept Penny away from Crosby Marlett's trap line because of the perils involved in haunting it, he himself had never held back on account of danger. Nor did he now.

Sean struck the line at the place he had left it earlier, sniffed at the snowshoe trail, discovered that the trapper had not been to visit his traps, and settled down to lope easily along the trail. Suddenly the snowshoe tracks left the old trail and turned up a brushy ridge. Sean followed.

Crosby Martlett was a good trapper and one who believed in sound trapping practices. He knew that foxes were at their best in the early part of the winter. As soon as the late-winter thaws set in, foxes liked to lie on sunny ledges and in other warm places. The sun bleached their fur, so that a late-caught fox was not worth one third as much as a pelt taken at the proper time. Crosby Marlett had stopped trapping foxes and was now working the thickets for wildcats and an occasional lynx. Wildcat pelts were worth little, but a ten-dollar bounty made them worth trapping. Lynx furs, still prime, found a ready market.

Sean swung aside to investigate a trap, found nothing in it, left it behind, and went on. The next set held a half-grown wildcat that unsheathed its claws and spat at him, but in the next was a snowshoe. Sean scratched snow and ice clods to spring the second trap of the set and then went in to take the big hare.

He ate it down to the last shred of meat, then for a while he lay up in a thicket. The big Setter rose from his nap to prowl restlessly about. He had already taken food to Penny, but she might be hungry again. Sean laid a halfhearted ambush for cottontails, succeeded in catching nothing, and swung back to Crosby Marlett's trap line. The third set he visited contained another snowshoe. The trapper baited his lynx and wildcat sets with meat upon which he put a drop or two of lure which he himself had invented. But the lure was equally fascinating to snowshoe hares. Since there were fifty of the big-footed crea-

tures for every wildcat, Marlett caught more hares
than anything else.

The snowshoe hanging from his jaws, Sean left the
trap line. He sought one of his regular routes to the
hemlock-bordered little creek, leaped to the mossy
boulder that divided the creek and sprang to the
opposite bank. Not once did he stop to look back or to
scout his back trail. The little hemlocks on both sides
of the creek grew so thickly that nothing could be
seen through them, and because no food grew within
the small trees nothing else was ever attracted to this
place. It was one of the very few ways that Sean had
full confidence in, and he had become so accustomed to coming this way in safety that now he seldom bothered to investigate.

He crossed the ridge upon which the pines grew
and swung toward the cave where Penny lay with
her pups. Suddenly he stopped.

Something was amiss; he did not quite know what.
There were no alien odors, but one of the pine
branches was swaying and swinging violently and
there was not enough wind to move it even gently.
Sean took a firmer grip on the snowshoe and ran full
speed toward the cave.

The den was silent, but Sean's nose told him that
Penny and the pups huddled in it. Penny, too, was
aware that a visitor had come to the pines and she
was ready for whatever might happen. She would
not leave the pups, but she was prepared to fight if
anything threatened them at the den's mouth. Sean
heard her warning snarl when he came near and
dropped the snowshoe.

The big Setter centered his attention on the pines,

now a scene of violent action. The black squirrel's endless practice leaps and complicated aerial maneuvers were paying off. The marten that he had long feared was finally here.

The squirrel raced up a limb, teetered for a split second on a supple twig that swayed and shook, and at exactly the right second he leaped. He caught himself on the very tip of another twig, scrambled for a hold, and raced down the limb.

Behind him the marten sprang across the same space and whisked after the squirrel. Only slightly larger than the quarry he pursued, the marten was as savage and as untiring as a mink or weasel. He was at home in trees and this was an old game to him. He knew that he could follow anywhere the squirrel might lead, and had the situation been even the marten would easily have overtaken his quarry.

The black squirrel had a slight advantage because of his endless practicing. He knew exactly every crossing he could leap and just how long it would take him to leap it. The pursuing marten had to test and feel his way, and every time he chased the squirrel from one tree into another he lost the fractional part of a second that gave the squirrel a priceless new start.

The squirrel raced up a big pine almost to the top. In the thin branches there he dodged and twisted, and sprang in a long descending curve that took him to a lower branch on another tree. The marten followed, not five leaps behind. Race at top speed, leaping from tree to tree, the black squirrel was tiring, and as he became weary the marten closed, inch by inch, the gap that separated them. The marten was almost upon him when the squirrel tried one last, desperate ruse.

He flung himself from the top of a tall pine, broke his fall by clawing at feathery twigs, bounced to the next limb, clawed a way to the trunk, and ran down it to the ground. Unwilling to follow a course so insane, the marten started straight down the trunk.

Dashing toward another tree, the black squirrel ran within a foot of Sean. Ordinarily the big Setter would have caught him—he could afford to overlook no source of food—but he knew the real danger here. Penny and the pups were in the cave. Although the squirrel would never harm them, the marten would gladly kill anything it could.

Sean bounced forward when the little killer was five feet away. Seeing him for the first time, the marten stopped so abruptly that he skidded on the snow. Recovering, he whirled and bounded back toward the tree he had just left. Sean leaped, closed his jaws over the marten, and sank his teeth deep. Carefully he pawed a hole in the snow and stuffed the dead marten in it. At the present time he was not hungry enough to eat a marten, but bitter experience had taught him to waste nothing.

High in one of the pines, the black squirrel crawled wearily into a nest and at once fell into the sleep of the utterly exhausted. Not again that day would he venture out.

Penny, satisfied that the danger was past, came out of the cave, picked up the snowshoe, and took it back with her. The pups were mewling and wailing as they sought to crowd each other away from their mother. Young as they were, while peril lurked near they had been satisfied to make no noise. But now the threat was past, and their only idea was to fill their bellies as full as possible.

Sean lay down in the pines, afraid to go near the den until Penny invited him to do so. The pups' squeaking and mewling made a faint chorus that could be heard above the whispering pines, but Sean remained unworried by the noise. Even if the pups attracted hungry things that would not hesitate to eat them, Penny was never more than a jump or two away from her babies and Sean had full confidence in her ability to take care of herself.

He rested while he could, for he knew that it would soon be time to go hunting again. Night had fallen, and the black squirrel in the tree had recovered from his fear when Sean started out to hunt.

As he crossed the meadow where he and Penny had leaped at and pulled down grouse, the black and white heifer glared truculently at him. The heifer had undergone her own misadventures while winter was running its course, and was not disposed to be friendly. Sean reminded her too much of Slasher, whom she had met on her travels.

All day and half the night the coy-dog had circled her, hoping for a killing stroke. But the heifer was very agile and much too strong for him. Always she faced him with flying hooves and raking horns, and had lived through a battle in which a tame cow would have died. The only marks were healing.

Sean chose a careful course around the embattled heifer. He had no quarrel with her, largely because he knew from inborn good sense what Slasher had had to find out by personal experience. The heifer was too big for any one dog or wolf to pull down. It would take a pack to get her, and then some of the pack would be almost sure to pay with their lives. The heifer was well able to take care of herself, and the big Setter knew it.

Sean trotted across the meadow and struck an angling course that took him back to Crosby Marlett's trap line. He stole a snowshoe from a trap, ate as much as he wanted, and carried the rest back to Penny.

Tired of the pups' innumerable demands, Penny came out of the den and sat for a while in the winter sunshine. She looked suspiciously at her mate, finally came close enough to sniff noses briefly, then flew back to the den in near panic when the pups began to mewl. When Sean ventured hopefully near, she set upon him and drove him back. He retreated to the usual distance and lay down.

Hunting was hard and he had a family to provide for. But as long as he could visit the traps he was assured of plenty. There were always snowshoes to be had and once he took Penny a wild turkey that had stepped into one of the traps and was struggling there.

Still, Sean instinctively realized that it was well not to go to the trap line too often. The pups were four days old when he varied his hunting routine by going into a rabbit thicket. He caught and ate a small cottontail, then ambushed one for Penny. It was hard work for small reward, and the next time they needed meat Sean returned to the trap line.

A little way from the trail, the Setter stopped in his tracks. His head was up, his nostrils questing. His nose told him that, hours ago, Crosby Marlett had come to visit his traps. After a few minutes, Sean went cautiously forward. He advanced haltingly, and stopped short when he came to the beaten trail.

Crosby Marlett had visited each one of his traps. He had taken the spitting little wildcat. Sean found its skinned carcass where the trapper had tossed it. Each of the traps from which Sean had wrenched snowshoes was reset. The big Setter felt his hackles rise, and within his mind suspicion mounted. Almost he was tempted to leave the line.

He did not because hunting for both Penny and himself was hard, and the easiest place to get all they needed was on the trap line. Besides, there was no sign of danger, no indication that the trapper had discovered Sean's raids or that he intended to do anything about them if he had. Sean padded quietly along Crosby Marlett's trail.

He stopped for a long time before the first trap that held a snowshoe, uncertain as to whether or not he should go in. There was nothing noticeably different from what he had always found. The big hare, trapped by both front paws, strained backward as far as it could go and sat still.

Sean circled, looking for a hidden trap or snare. He found none, but still stood for a long while, studying the situation. Nothing threatened. At the same time, he was warned of an unseen, unknown thing that he could neither smell, nor see, nor hear. He could only sense a hidden menace.

Again, making sure of exactly where he placed each paw, he circled. The trap chain rattled when the snowshoe jumped suddenly. Kicking with powerful hind paws, it leaped clear across the set, only to find that it could go no farther. The chain was short, the steel jaws relentless. Panting, the hare crouched where it landed.

Sean went in swiftly, snapping with his big jaws even as he lunged. He seized the snowshoe, wrenched it loose from the trap, and leaped sideways, all in the same motion. Safely away from the trap, he turned to look back at it. Nothing had happened. There remained only the sensation that something might have happened.

The snowshoe hanging from his jaws, Sean faded away from the trap line. Crosby Marlett had come and gone, as his scent proved, but still the sense of concealed danger lingered. Sean dove into the laurel, running straight and fast. He still could not rid himself of the feeling that something was not as it should be.

Even the thickly growing little hemlocks that bordered the gurgling stream seemed to be no shelter. Sean halted, dropped the snowshoe, and stood with both front paws on it while he tested the wind currents. They bore no hint of anything amiss.

Sean took the snowshoe in his jaws again and walked slowly on his usual path toward the little stream. There was nothing here that he had not seen a hundred times before. He could smell the usual woodland odors. There was not the faintest sign of man, and Sean feared nothing else. The big Setter leaped from the hemlock-bordered bank onto the rock around which the stream divided.

His descending right front paw landed squarely in

a wolf trap that leaped up and clutched him with
steel jaws.

For a moment, after the steel clamped on his paw,
Sean held perfectly still while the rushing water
surged around the rock. He did not, as any animal
with an unstable temperament would have done, fly
into a writhing panic that would have succeeded
only in grinding the trap's jaws deeper into his paw.
He did not even drop the snowshoe he carried.

When he did let go of the big hare, he laid it
carefully on the boulder. Then, his mouth empty,
Sean limped on three legs to ease the pain and pressure in his trapped paw. Intently he studied the trap
on his foot. He tried to bite it with his jaws, and knew
as soon as he tried that his teeth were no match for
such a thing.

Sean sat down while the water curled around his
rear and banked up to soak his belly. He tried a
sudden, strong leap that only brought him up with a
sharp jerk. For a second he struggled furiously, not
panic-stricken but merely trying with strength and
force to rid himself of the thing on his foot. He
couldn't do it. The trap was stronger than he.

Wet fur plastered close against his body, his long
hair dripping icy water, Sean bent his head to look
again at the trap. It was a puzzle, a cold and unyielding thing with no life or being of its own. He had
already discovered that he could not rend it with his
jaws or pull himself out of it. Still, there must be a
way.

He laid his trapped paw on the boulder, beside the
dead hare. Carefully he pulled the big snowshoe

over the trap, so that it was completely hidden. He tried to walk away. When he did, the trap came with him. Apparently it could not be hidden. Sean nosed his swelling paw, and licked it gently with a warm tongue.

Suddenly he tensed himself and bristled. The eddying winds had brought to him the faint scent of man.

Sean sat down on the boulder and waited. Fear and uncertainty tore at him. He had a great desire to run, but he could not because the trap held him fast. Five minutes later he saw the man.

Billy Dash stood framed in the hemlocks.

11. Night Journey

When Billy Dash went back to his cabin he was puzzled. Crosby Marlett certainly knew the signs of a trap-line pirate, and Billy was not definitely sure whether the track he had seen was that of a dog or wolf. They were so very much alike that even experts couldn't always tell the difference. But there were just some things that didn't add up.

Wolves were wary, probably warier than anything else. In the ordinary course of events they wouldn't come within a hundred yards of anything that looked like a trap or smelled like one. Yet, a trap-line robber most surely knew that he was stealing from traps. The robber *must* be an outlaw dog.

Billy stared hard at the wall of his little cabin. He saw visions of the past, of the happy times when he had worked with Danny Pickett and the Irish Setters.

Dogs turned outlaw for a reason, and some man's mishandling usually lay behind it. Billy looked hungrily at the wall. It would be nice to have a dog, any dog at all, to share his exile. Of course it would be a breach of their agreement if he trespassed on Crosby Marlett's trap line, and a serious offense if he interfered with any of Crosby's traps. Still, Billy knew that he had to go to find out for himself.

The next morning he pushed cautiously through the little hemlocks that bordered Fordyce Creek. He knew the place, even to the rock Crosby had mentioned. Almost he turned and went back. This was an unfair trick to be playing on a man who had been a friend when Billy was in desperate need of one. But he could not help going on.

When Billy saw Sean his heart seemed to stop beating. Nothing of Sean's misadventures was known to him, and he could not have been more astounded if he had run across an elephant here in this northern wilderness. Rooted in his tracks, Billy saw the dead snowshoe on the rock and guessed where it had come from.

When he did advance he went slowly, feasting his eyes upon the dog who, since Billy had first seen him, had filled his dreams. There was no logical explanation as to how he had come here, but here he was.

"Hello, Dog," Billy said softly.

Sean was dazed. For a long while he had run loose in the woods, with no one except himself to depend upon. He had faced dangers and triumphed over them. Now, suddenly, he was face to face with the man to whom he would gladly have devoted every beat of the strong heart within him. He had met the being whom he could revere above all others, and the numbing shock of the encounter left him unnerved.

At the same time, he was months removed from the prize-winning dog who had romped so gaily with Billy Dash. Sean had become a wild thing. He had suffered hurt and rebuff. He had won a mate, and had become the provider for her and the pups, who were waiting for him back in the pine grove.

He retreated as far as the trap chain would let him go when Billy Dash came near, and a warning growl rumbled from his throat. It was not the snarl that would have ripped forth had Jake Busher or Crosby Marlett found him helpless. Sean growled because he could not help it. He did not want to hurt Billy Dash, but at the same time he must protect himself.

"I know, Dog," Billy said. "But I don't think you really mean it."

Never moving fast, and never making an indecisive motion, Billy stepped into the little creek and waded toward Sean. The big Setter, watching him come, calculated the time to launch himself at Billy's throat. But he could not force himself to spring.

Gently, soothingly, Billy's supple fingers slid down Sean's trapped leg.

The dog opened his big jaws, closed them over Billy's arm, and pinched until the ends of his teeth met flesh. Sean did not bite any deeper. He rolled his eyes, wanting to see how Billy would take this. He heard Billy laugh softly.

"Youah not goin' to bite me, Dog."

Sean opened his jaws. His body was tense as a fiddle string, his brain a seething whirl, when Billy lifted his trapped paw and gently laid it across his knee. His strong hands depressed both trap springs. The trap slid from his paw and Sean was free.

He knew it, but he made no instantaneous move to leap aside and put himself out of harm's way. Instead, he lifted his great head to stare straight at Billy. Billy Dash looked back, and in that second there passed between them something that very few dogs and masters ever know. It was as though, by some magical process, each was able to communicate his thoughts to the other.

"Go ahead, Dog," said Billy sadly.

He looked again at the snowshoe. Dogs running wild were not in the habit of carrying their food around with them until such time as they saw fit to eat. They hunted because they were hungry, and as soon as they caught something they ate it. Obviously, somewhere back in the brush, Sean had a mate and a family. Beyond doubt, Billy decided, the big Setter had taken up with a coyote or a wolf.

Sean took a step forward, picked up the snowshoe, and looked around. He leaped to the opposite bank, turned around to look once more at Billy Dash, then faded into the hemlocks. He had his choice and he had made it.

Billy swallowed the terrific lump in his throat and turned slowly away. He knew that he was in trouble. Billy had not made the slightest effort to hide his trail or conceal his actions, and Crosby Marlett was an expert at reading signs. He would know not only that his trap had been tampered with but also who had done it. Crosby would not forgive such a thing. He had been determined to kill the trap-line robber, and the fact that it was a dog would make no difference.

Billy went back to his cabin, prepared a supper for which he had little appetite, and made his decision.

Crosby Marlett had run this line yesterday. Since he ran it only every fourth day, he would not be back for two more days. When he came, Billy decided, he would meet him at Allerton Creek, explain what he had done, why he had done it, and let Crosby take any action he saw fit.

Sean was troubled and restless as he trotted toward the pines. Because he was a dog, without a human's powers of reasoning, it never once occurred to him that there might be a satisfactory solution to his problem. Torn between a great desire to follow Billy Dash and a greater one to return to Penny, he had done what his deepest instincts told him to do. He did not think beyond that. It would be possible to take Penny and the pups to Billy Dash or to bring Billy to them, but Sean did not reason that far.

He was so disturbed that he became careless and ventured too close to the den. Penny dashed out to rake him with punishing teeth. Sean dropped the snowshoe, yelped, and fled like a chastised puppy. Tail between his legs, still-damp ears flattened against his head, he stopped only when Penny left him and returned to the cave.

Sean turned to look at her, and lay down in the pines. But not for long could he stay quiet. His paws twitched nervously and his tail wagged as pleasant memories of Billy Dash chased one another through his head. He did not take notice even when Silverwing, who had at last returned to the pines, dropped a cone on his head.

Sean padded back and forth. Again he approached the den, only to have Penny fly out and chase him away. Sean retreated to his proper distance, and turned to look back at the cave. Then he could no longer control himself.

Penny was his love and his life. He had chosen her

and he would not leave her. Yet he had to know more about Billy Dash, even though he had no intention of meeting him again. There was that about the man which the big Setter just could not resist, and he set out from the pine grove because he was unable to help himself.

He raced back to the little stream and crossed it, wading cautiously around the boulder. His tail wagged, at first jerkily and then happily, as he picked up Billy Dash's scent. Sean was not a trailing dog insofar as he had never learned to trail game. But any good dog can always find his master by trailing him, and Billy Dash's scent was very plain on the snow.

Sean stopped to test the breezes, then swung in the direction Billy Dash had taken, straight into the wilderness. Stopping for nothing, Sean followed the trail. His tail wagged almost constantly and there was a look of sheer happiness in his eyes. He crossed and paid no attention to the fresh scents of snow-shoes and cottontails. Once he bristled, paused to sniff briefly at the track of a lynx, and sped on. There was only one goal that interested him now.

Night had come and the first quarter of a thin moon rode in the sky when Sean broke out of some sparse beeches that straggled along the top of a low, rocky ridge. Below him was a valley which rose on the opposite side to another low ridge. The smell of wood smoke hung heavily in the air, and Sean quivered excitedly.

Billy Dash's trails and paths were everywhere. Whining under his breath, Sean trotted down the slope. Shielded by the friendly darkness, he halted twenty feet from the cabin's door. Varied smells wafted about, but predominating was the fresh scent of the man he had been following. So tense that his muscles ached, Sean sat perfectly still. Then, slowly, carefully putting one paw in front of the other, he walked toward the cabin.

At the rear was a window, a single pane of glass through which flowed yellow light from a kerosene lamp. For a moment Sean paused beneath that window. Finally he raised himself effortlessly, put both front paws on the sill, and looked in.

His back to the window, Billy Dash was busy at the old iron stove that occupied the far end of the single room. Satisfied, Sean dropped from the window and raced into the night.

From a safe distance away, he turned to look back. Not a second time did he turn his head. The big Setter must return to Penny and the pups. He did not walk or trot now, but raced with the effortless, mile-eating, tireless lope of an Irish Setter.

A half mile from the den he halted. Sean's hackles rose, his lips lifted from polished fangs, and he gave one rippling, savage snarl. Before him in the snow was the smoking-hot trail of Slasher. Far too close to Penny and the pups, the killer had come this way not five minutes past.

12. The Feud

Sean bounded across the night-frozen crust, leaping the logs and stumps in his path and crashing through brush. He turned aside only for whatever he could not go through or over. For the first time in his life, he was afraid. But not for himself.

He knew Slasher far better than any man can ever hope to know any animal. Sean's was a beast's understanding, uncolored by sentiment or false assumptions. Slasher was a dangerous, vindictive killer, a hybrid that was neither all dog nor all coyote, and therefore outcast by both. Belonging to nothing, loved by nothing, he found an outlet in viciousness and bitter hatred of everything that moved.

Should he find Penny and the pups before Sean got to them, Slasher would at once seek a fight. Penny would defend her babies, but only the biggest and strongest dog could hope to defeat Slasher. Penny could not. She was thirty pounds lighter than Sean, and though she had great courage, the odds would be hopeless. Penny and the pups would die if Slasher found them first.

Sean whimpered anxiously as he raced along at top speed. Slasher was heading directly up the ridge that flanked the grove of pine trees. The prevailing winds were sweeping upward out of the valley, so he could not help getting Penny's scent. Sean leaped a huge fallen pine, balanced himself on the other side, and only with the barest whisk of a pause to regain his equilibrium, he sped on. He was running a race with death itself, and knew it.

He abandoned all attempts to follow Slasher's trail and took a direct course for the cave, one that led him through a blackberry thicket. Thorned blackberry canes tore at him as he raced. He left tufts of hair on all the bushes but gave the raking canes no more attention than he would have paid to so many willow withes.

Sean burst into the pine grove so fast and so angrily that Silverwing and his mate, awakened from sound sleep, took raucous flight. Reaching the pines, the big Setter stood still, one forepaw lifted and nose questing. His body was stiff, his tail curved in a half circle behind him. Sean knew that Penny and the pups were safe, because the wind told him so. Now he strove for some concrete evidence of Slasher.

He knew the killer was there on the ridge, only a little distance away. But the wind swept out of the valley and straight up the slope. He could smell nothing on the ridge. He mounted a boulder to see if he could get a different breeze a little higher up. Still the winds came out of the valley.

There was motion at the den's mouth and Penny came out to stand beside him. She could smell nothing and she had heard nothing, but she knew from her mate's actions that some deadly danger was near. Somewhere out in the wilderness was something so terrible and so vicious that even Sean was afraid of it. Penny trembled and pressed close to his side. It was all very well to drive him away from the pups, and, as a mother with babies to defend, it was Penny's right to do this. But in a real emergency he was still her staunch defender.

Penny looked sideways at Sean. When he paid no attention to her she trotted softly back to the den, where the nine squirming pups crawled over her. Penny stopped trembling, contented because Sean was there. He was a safe bulwark against anything that might come.

Sean stood still as a carved statue on his boulder. Fierce rage replaced the combined anger and fear he had known; anger at Slasher's presence and fear for Penny and the pups. Now he was here, and anything that threatened his family would first have to kill him.

He was nervous and anxious, because he could see, hear, and smell nothing out of the ordinary. But he was so familiar with the winds and their tricks that he knew why that was. And he was deadly certain that Slasher was on the ridge.

Sean was sure because the past months had made him aware of the ways of wild things. A deer, following the same path Slasher had taken, would have gone up the ridge. So would a bear, a wildcat, or anything else that was not running from an enemy. The ridge was simply the easiest and most logical way to travel. It was the way Sean himself would have selected had he not been so anxious to reach the den. Slasher could not be elsewhere.

The winds waned, shifted a little, and Sean corroborated with his nose what he had known to be the truth. Faint, but certain, he caught the coy-dog's hated scent. It came with a puff of wind and was gone almost immediately, but unmistakably it had been there.

Sean raised his head and gave voice to a great battle roar. It was a thunderous, rolling blast, a challenge directed at anything within hearing but primarily at Slasher. Hearing it, Penny curled her head to enfold the pups in a warm arc made by her own body, and felt reassured. The two ravens, down over the rim of the hill, huddled close together and were silent. In a leafy nest, the black squirrel opened his eyes and stirred uncomfortably.

Sean's roar was thousands of years old, something that had descended through the mists of time. The first dog that had been called upon to defend its mate and young from a prowling saber-tooth tiger or dire wolf had issued the same call to fight and so had all dogs since, when they found themselves in similar circumstances. It was not a pack cry, but the proud, single voice of one strong creature. It informed all within hearing that he was willing and able to protect what he held most dear.

The final echoes of his challenge still haunted the forest when Sean leaped from his boulder and sought a place close to the den. He had flung his boast to the whole world, he had said that he was strongest, and now let Slasher try to prove otherwise. Sean was ready.

But Slasher did not show himself, because he was too wise for that. He could stand and kill two winded hounds that were supposed to kill him. He killed sheep and calves whenever he could do so without danger to himself because it was his nature to kill.

But Slasher was no fool. He had fought Sean once before and he knew the big Setter as a formidable antagonist. For Penny alone he had only contempt, but Penny and Sean together would wage a ferocious battle. As they stood, the odds were heavier than Slasher liked.

A past master of wild strategy, Slasher knew how to take perfect advantage of the winds, and had no intention of letting Sean and Penny know all about him. He circled the den, always being careful to stay downwind, and after a little while he left to hunt.

Sean maintained his sentry post, and again Penny came out to sniff noses briefly with him. She retreated when the pups started mewling, and growled when Sean came near. Sean padded to the edge of the slope and looked down it.

He had to hunt because Penny needed food, but there could be no more thought of going back to Crosby Marlett's trap line. It was too far. Slasher could slip in, do his deadly work, and be gone before Sean returned. Still, there had to be something to eat.

Sean slipped down the slope, laid an ambush in a rabbit thicket, and caught a small cottontail. He carried it back to the den, watched Penny come out to take it, and resumed his sentry duty while she ate. Not for a moment did he dare relax. The eddying breezes had carried no recent scent of Slasher, but the killer knew of the cave and that was enough.

Hungry, but not daring to hunt for himself unless the situation became desperate, Sean dozed near the den. Even while he slept, his nostrils tested and analyzed every little breeze. Should one bring any alien or dangerous scent, Sean would be on his feet in the wink of an eye and ready for anything.

The afternoon sun was waning when he went forth to hunt again. The pups were crying and Penny, hungry, was restless. Sean slipped back to the same thicket where he had caught the cottontail and settled himself in an ambush.

Like thin notes from a bugle, Penny's shrill yelp of anger floated down the slope to him. Penny gave voice again, a high-pitched sound of sheerest rage, and Sean sprang erect. He bounded back up the slope and into the pines.

Hackles raised, fangs bared, Penny stood in front of the cave. The heavy scent of Slasher was all about. But he had fled, his trail ending a hundred feet from Penny.

Sean paused long enough to assure himself that Penny and the pups had not been harmed, then he took the battle upon himself. This had to be ended, and it could end only with the death of Slasher or himself. If Penny became hungry enough, the frozen marten was still buried where Sean had left it. Before he brought more food to his family, Sean had an enemy to hunt.

He struck Slasher's trail and hurried along it. The killer must be pushed hard; any errors on Sean's part and the coy-dog would have ample time to slip back to the den. There could be no mistakes.

All night long and until the early hours of the morning, Billy Dash fretted in his cabin. He had been all right, sure of himself and what he was going to do, until he had again run across Sean. Then, with cruel force, all the dreams of what might have been came out of the dark shadows to torment him again.

Working for Danny Pickett, Billy had never once asked himself whether a kennel boy had a high or a low station in life. He didn't care. What had mattered, and all that had mattered, was the fact that he had worked with Irish Setters. There was something about such dogs that represented to Billy what a collector's finest paintings mean to him. And Sean seemed to him the finest in the collection.

More than once Billy had dreamed that Sean was his dog. If only he had been, Billy felt, he would have envied nobody else in the entire world. Sean had great intelligence, which Billy had appreciated from the first, and a magnificent body. Above and beyond that he had a certain independence of spirit that set him apart.

It had never occurred to Billy, when he had Sean alone and helpless in a trap, that he might have overwhelmed him with force, tied him up, and made him do whatever Billy wished. You just didn't try that with dogs like Sean any more than you tried it with a certain type of man. Sean had a mind and a will of his own. It might be possible to subdue him with clubs and whips, and to break his spirit, but if that were done Sean would no longer be Sean. He would be just a dog.

A dozen times Billy lay down on his bunk, and a dozen times he got up. Everything was blurred and distorted in his mind. Morning light glowed through the cabin's frosted window when Billy lay down again, and this time sheer weariness forced him into deep slumber.

Morning was well under way when he awakened to a loud knock on the cabin's door. At once the dream world of a magnificent Irish Setter named Sean faded away and the stern realities of Billy Dash's world came back. It must be the Police.

Billy glanced toward the .45 hanging in its holster from a wooden peg driven into the cabin's wall. At once he put the thought aside. He had shot Uncle Hat, accidentally. Never, if he could help it, would he shoot anyone deliberately. He had known the risks he ran when he decided to take his chances in the wilderness. Apparently he had gambled and lost.

The knock was repeated, louder, and Billy Dash swung from his bunk. He slipped into his clothing, thrust his feet into unlaced boots, and looked around the cabin. The window was too small for him to climb through, and the cabin had only one door. Like Sean, he had been caught in a trap.

Billy walked to the door, opened it, and stood face to face with Crosby Marlett and Danny Pickett.

For a moment he stood in shocked surprise. He had expected the Police. Instead, he saw two of the very few human beings whom he had ever trusted completely. Danny broke the silence.

"Hello, Billy."

"Hi."

"Are you going to ask us in?"

"Uh—shuah. Come on in."

They entered, and Billy closed the door against the frigid air. There was another awkward silence.

"I brought him here, Billy," Crosby Marlett said.

"That's right," Danny seconded. "Crosby brought me. But he didn't really give you away; he just slipped. I met him in Cedar Run last night and he started telling me about a trap-line outlaw. 'Billy Dash,' Crosby said, 'thinks it's a dog.' So I told him about Hat Dash, and how there's no sense in your hiding out now, and he brought me over here."

"You mean Uncle Hat isn't—"

"No, Hat's not dead; guess he's too ornery to kill." Danny grinned. "When Hat got out of the hospital, he swore up and down that you asked him to come see you and, as soon as he came, you grabbed the .45 and let him have it."

"Sounds like Uncle Hat."

"It is like him, but there are others who know better. Both Dad and I know where your pay was found; the State Police have figured out for themselves what happened. They had long talks with Hat. You'll have to face trial, maybe, but Mr. Haggin said he'll have his own lawyers defend you and there'll be nothing to it. You can have your old job back, too. How about it?"

In spite of his relief, all the old doubts and fears welled up in Billy at mention of a trial. Any Dash who mixed with the law always came out second best. Promises, even promises from Danny Pickett, meant little when you were a Dash and in trouble. Billy wavered uncertainly. It would be mighty nice to be back with Danny, but . . .

Seeing Billy's troubled face, Danny abruptly changed the subject.

"Now about this trap-line robber you think is a dog. Did you know Sean was gone?"

"Uh—Sean?"

Danny spoke meaningly. "You remember him?"

"Oh, shuah! Shuah! I'll nevah fo'get Sean!"

"I didn't think you would. We sent him over to Tom Jordan's last summer. He spilled out the back end of the truck and—"

"And you nevah found him."

"How do you know that?"

"Would you be heah lookin' fo' him if you had?"

"One for you, Billy. I found his crate and looked all over the place for him. I couldn't find him. Then I got word of a big red outlaw raiding Jake Busher's sheep."

Crosby Marlett said, "They all turn outlaw when they go wild. There's no good in 'em any more."

Billy Dash gave the trapper a glance. "How come you didn't know about this outlaw dog, Crosby?"

"I got no sheep and I mind my own business. But now I think you're right and it is a dog. I had him in the trap on Fordyce Crick, but he pulled out before we got there."

Billy said nothing. Obviously Crosby Marlett hadn't studied the sign very carefully or he would have known that Sean had not pulled out of the trap by himself. Well, Crosby might and might not go back for a second and closer look.

"I figured he'd be hanging around Jake Busher's," Danny said, "or else close to Jordan's. Never thought he'd come this far. He's got a mate in here somewhere."

"How do you know?" Billy challenged.

Danny asked, "Do you know that one of Tom Jordan's prize Irish Setters, Penny, was lured away last fall?"

This time Billy was really surprised. "I didn't know that."

"You know it now. How long have you been here?"

"All wintah."

"And you never saw any sign of an outlaw dog?"

Billy Dash said forcefully, "So help me, I nevah even saw the footprint of an *outlaw* dog!"

"That's an odd thing; maybe he hasn't crossed into your territory. Still, I think this is Sean, Billy. If he'd been bad hurt in the fall he wouldn't have gone very far from the crate; I'd have found some sign. Besides, it all adds up. I should have figured it before. Sean's turned outlaw, he's here, and he's got Penny with him."

"That's a lot to guess at."

"I'd still bet on it. Sean didn't bring Penny directly here. As long as they could track him on the snow, he swung clear away. That's where they've been hunting him, far to the south. And that's one more reason why I'm sure that it's Sean. He planned to outsmart any trackers and he did. Why, he got away from the best hound pack Jack Busher could round up."

Billy Dash bit his lower lip in sudden anger. He, too, knew what it was like to be hunted.

"Why don't you let him be?" he said fiercely.

Danny faced him squarely, and Billy looked nervously away. It seemed, in that moment, that Danny Pickett knew a lot, or had guessed a lot, that he was not telling Crosby Marlett. And maybe Danny understood a great deal more than Billy thought he did.

Danny said, "There's a lot of dog there, Billy, and a lot of money and hope tied up in him."

"Youah tellin' me he's a lot of dog!"

"I'll change that. He used to be a lot of dog."

"What do you mean by that?"

"He's an outlaw now. You know the usual end of outlaws."

Billy Dash's voice was cold. "Maybe I do. Maybe I don't."

"There's one thing sure; Sean and Penny have a family somewhere. That adds up too; no dog raids a trap line and drags off what he finds there for himself alone. The least we aim to do is get Penny and the pups, and we can do that right now."

Crosby Marlett nodded. "They won't be too far off. If we pick up that dog's tracks where he crossed Fordyce Crick, they should take us some'ere."

Danny was too casual. "We'll catch Sean, too, if we can. If we can't, if he tries to protect Penny and the pups, we may have to get rough. I don't aim to have my throat ripped out by any dog, not even Sean."

"You can't shoot him!" Billy cried.

"I wouldn't like to." Danny paused. "Why don't you come along with us? He was always your dog more than he was anyone else's. He might listen to you."

"Suppose he won't?"

"Billy, I promise, if you can get Sean back, he's yours."

"Mine!"

"That's right. All Mr. Haggin asks are the pups."

Billy's head whirled. That he should come even close to owning Sean! It was far too much to imagine all at once. But first they had to find the big Setter.

"All right," he said. "If you really mean it." He threw what cooked food he had into his pack sack, added a blanket, and picked up his old lumberman's jacket. "Let's go."

They picked up Sean's trail on the far side of Fordyce Creek. It was hard to follow, and it could not have been followed except by men who knew all about trails. Guiding themselves by faint marks in the snow, bent or broken twigs, a scuffed mark on a moss-covered boulder, Danny and Crosby Marlett led off. Billy followed, hating himself for having any part in this raid on Sean's family, but knowing it would be made whether he came along or not.

Two hours after they left Fordyce Creek, they stood on the ridge above the pine grove. Silverwing and his mate, seeing men approach, took hasty flight. Penny's subdued snarl rolled from the cave and, when they came near, she rushed out. Bristling, fangs bared, she took a ready stance in front of the den.

But never in her whole life had Penny been hurt by any man; had Sean not prevented her she would have gone back to Jordan's long ago. And Danny Pickett had a way with Irish Setters. He advanced steadily, talking to Penny as he did so, while her threatening snarls subsided to a rumbling growl.

Then, suddenly, the transformation was complete. Penny was again a man's dog. She stood anxiously, but proudly, while Danny crawled into the den and caught the wriggling pups. He held up a big, strong pup in one hand and grinned at Billy Dash.

"Look. Still think Sean had nothing to do with it?"

"Wondeh wheah he is?"

"He's an outlaw," Crosby Marlett grunted. "He's run away."

Danny made a cradle of his coat, laid all the pups in it, and gathered them in his arms. Penny stood near, her silken head raised toward the pups as she crowded anxiously at Danny's side.

"Coming, Billy?" Danny asked.

Billy Dash souffed the snow with the toe of his pac. "No. I'm goin' to look for Sean,"

"Don't be a fool!" Crosby snorted. "The only way you'll get that dog is with a trap or a gun."

Danny smiled to himself, but nodded soberly. "You may be right. Good luck, anyway, Billy. And don't forget there's a place at the Picketts' for a reformed outlaw—or even two of 'em."

13. The Battle

Over the ridge and down the other side Sean raced. Slasher was running straight away from the den; the wily killer knew that he was pursued. He had not yet made up his mind whether or not to fight. When and if he did, the battle would take place in an arena of Slasher's choice.

The afternoon waned into night. Pale stars glittered, and a thin moon climbed slowly into the sky. Sean ran swiftly, nose to the snow. They were in broken country now, a wild and weird place of narrow little gullies and cliffs. Black rocks that had never been snow-covered because fierce winds whipped all snow away from them, were irregularly spaced, like a parade of frozen mummies.

Sean stretched his legs harder, for Slasher's scent was now hot in his nostrils. Fierce anger burned within the big Setter. Tongue lolling, he dashed through the mouth of a narrow little gully that was flanked on both sides by sheer rock walls. Too late, he whirled to defend himself.

Like a grotesque bird in the night, Slasher rose from the top of the rock wall and hurled himself out and down. His aim was perfect. Squarely on top of Sean he landed, and as he did his jaws snaked toward the place where Sean's neck met his skull.

Slasher, who had doubled back for an ambush, had every intention of ending this fight before it fairly began.

Sean had no time to think. Only the fact that he was running, and that Slasher misjudged his speed a hair's breadth, saved his life. Sean spilled forward on his chin, and instead of biting through the spine, Slasher's fangs sliced through Sean's shoulder.

The big Setter's breath left him in a great, whooshing gasp. His chin collided sharply with the crust and his hindquarters flew into the air. The advantage remained with Slasher. He had missed the first time, but he had a second chance. With deadly purpose he lunged in to strike again at Sean's neck. Once more he misjudged.

Slasher had never run with a pack, but his strongest instincts and his most dependable methods were pack methods. In a pack hunt, any quarry that went down and stayed down was immediately overwhelmed by a whole tangle of furry bodies and literally ripped apart by razor-sharp teeth. Slasher had based his second strike on the assumption that Sean would immediately get to his feet.

Instead, the big Setter rolled over on his back and folded his paws so that they would not make a good target. It was a planned move, a fighter's ruse, but only the trickiest and most intelligent dog or wolf would have dared try it. To do so incorrectly was to put one's self at the mercy of the enemy. To do it correctly was to find one of the best possible positions for striking back.

When Slasher came in, Sean used his supple back as a focal point, and rolled. At the same time he raised his big head, snapped, and felt his teeth meet through the fleshy part of Slasher's left shoulder. Almost at once he relinquished the hold, and never stopped his rolling motion. When Sean ended up he was back on his feet.

In the narrow little gully, scarcely six feet at its widest, the dog and the half-dog faced each other, tense and strangely silent. Their paws were braced, their jaws ready. Neither knew any fear and neither thought of running. This was to be a finish fight.

Like a gliding snake Slasher came forward. He did not move fast and he uttered no sound. Slasher had had all the initial advantage. He had been unable to keep it and now, if possible, he must regain the upper hand.

As Sean met him unflinchingly, out of that earlier time when he had fought this same enemy certain memories came to his aid. Slasher's style of fighting was never to close unless he could see some definite opening, and before he risked hurt to himself he must be fairly certain that he could inflict greater hurt on his enemy. Sean remembered that.

Slasher was a yard way when Sean lunged forward. The first time he met Slasher he had been soft-muscled, a kennel dog that had no real opportunity for the exercise he needed. Running in the forest had removed the last trace of fat and flabbiness. Sean had kept his weight, but now it was hard flesh and supple muscle. The constant practice which he had had in the bitter struggle just to survive had given him superb control.

But Slasher was as big and as strong as Sean, and definitely no amateur when it came to fighting. Incredibly fast, lithe as a dancer, he twisted away from Sean's attack and whirled to see if there was an opportunity to launch one of his own. Slasher, too, remembered their former battle and knew something about Sean's style of fighting. Now he waited patiently for Sean to make a mistake. Then would come Slasher's time to kill.

Like trained boxers they circled and shifted, each watching the other and each trying to catch the other unguarded. Then they came together, two furred, fierce beasts that were blind to everything except the battle. They parted with almost no damage done. Both had striven for a killing blow. Both were so expert at parrying and thrusting that neither had found anything except a mouthful of hair.

Slasher leaped in, straight at Sean's chest, and Sean braced to meet him. But at the final second Slasher swerved aside. His shearing teeth left long wounds on Sean's ribs, and then the coy-dog was gone. Sean, counterslashing, got only another mouthful of gray fur.

Sean gave a little ground, and was ready when Slasher repeated the maneuver. He swerved at the same time, and their heads met. Muzzle to muzzle they stood, their wildly gnashing teeth sounding like a series of steel traps snapping in fast succession. Both were torn and bleeding now, although neither had a crippling wound.

For the space of two minutes they circled each other while the pale moon waned under the half light of early dawn. Again they met in a writhing tangle of furred bodies and snapping teeth.

The dog and the coy-dog were panting now, jaws

wide open and tongues lolling full length as they
continued their ferocious duel. Sean dipped his
head briefly to soothe his hot tongue against cold
snow. Seeing his enemy off guard, Slasher undu-
lated across the space that separated them.

As Sean side-stepped to repel the attack, Slasher
crowded him against the gully's wall. Sean fought
back, giving blow for blow, until Slasher dived suddenly. So low that he had to spread both front paws
on the snow, he pushed himself along with his hind
legs while his wolfish head went in fast. His jaws
found Sean's right front leg, and there was the sound
of cracking bone as they closed on it.

Slasher leaped back, and everything was over;
Sean limped on three legs. None knew better than
Slasher that the strike might as well have been the
fatal one. A three-legged creature cannot possibly
fight as hard or maneuver as fast as one that has free
use of all four legs. Now it was only a matter of time.

The coy-dog danced a bit to one side, made a lunge
at Sean's left front foot, and withdrew. Again he
feinted, and again withdrew. Certain of victory now,
he began a slow, determined attack.

Sean gave ground, his muscles limp and his body
loose. With only three usable legs he could not parry
and slash with the lightning speed that this fight
demanded. Nor could he run even if he had wanted
to.

The coy-dog's advance was steady and unwaver-
ing. His purpose was to rush in at the proper second
and, in rushing, to overwhelm Sean. He needed only
one more good opportunity. With all the power of his

hard muscles and sinewy body he went in for the finish.

This was what Sean had expected and what he had been looking for. He knew the rush was coming and timed it precisely, but he did not try to meet Slasher on his feet. Instead, with the killer's jaws within an inch of his throat, Sean threw himself down and rolled over on his back. His timing could not have been more perfect.

Slasher had expected to meet a solidly braced body. He met no resistance whatever, and his own momentum carried him on and over. He missed his strike at Sean's throat and, instead of bearing Sean down, he straddled him.

Sean raised his head and clamped his mighty jaws over Slasher's lean belly. His teeth sliced through muscle and sinew to Slasher's vital organs. The big Setter slashed again, swifter than any eye could follow, and a split second later he rolled sideways, rose on three legs, and faced Slasher.

His face a snarling mark of hate, Slasher gave voice to his rage for the first time. But they were bubbly growls that had nothing in them except a threat that Slasher could no longer carry out. In that one brief second when he had been able to do so, Sean had bitten deeply and hard. His hindquarters sagging, Slasher could no longer move at anything except a dragging walk. His strength was ebbing fast.

For two seconds more, when Sean went in, Slasher tried to meet him with strike for strike. Then he went down, and when Sean moved away Slasher stayed down. His front paws twitched spasmodically, but other than that he did not move. Slasher, the killer, was dead.

Sean looked at him for a long moment, wanting to assure himself that his enemy would not get up again. When he did not, Sean turned and limped toward the mouth of the gully. His task was finished. He was free to return to Penny and the pups.

His many wounds were very painful, and after a quarter of a mile he stopped to lick them. When he tried to catch his weight on the broken front foot, the bones grated sickeningly, but Sean did not cry out. Curling his paw, he stopped trying to lick his hurts and limped on three feet.

Again and again he had to stop to rest, and at no time could he travel swiftly. Twilight was gathering over the pine grove when Sean approached it. As soon as he was close enough to read with his nose the story of what had happened there, he tried to hurry.

Plain in the pine grove were the scents of three men he knew: Billy Dash, Danny Pickett, and Crosby Marlett. But Sean knew even before he entered the pine grove that Penny and the pups were not there. His home had been raided, his family was gone. Sean limped slowly to the mouth of the cave and stood there, trembling. His head drooped so low that his nose almost brushed the snow's crust. He had won the battle, but he had lost everything else. Suddenly he halted. The wind was again sweeping out of the valley and up the ridge, so that Sean could get no clear scent from the pines on the ridge. He was weary to the point of exhaustion and he was heartsick. Just the same, he knew there was something else in the grove.

"Hello, Dog," a soft voice said.

Half-hidden in the gathering twilight, Billy Dash stood in the pines a little way off. He made no effort to move nearer, and Sean made none to run away.

The big Setter stood still, puzzled and not at all sure what to do. His first obligation was to Penny and the pups, but Penny and the pups were gone. They had been taken away by men whom he knew and who had never harmed him. And another, the one who had won his devotion in his kennel days, was still there.

Billy Dash said, "It's up to you, Dog."

The voice, and the presence, finally touched the proper chord in Sean. His misery and heartbreak faded, and his cuts and aches were momentarily forgotten. He limped slowly across the snow toward Billy Dash, and unhesitatingly laid his head on Billy's knee. Billy Dash's voice shook.

"I thought you'd come back heah, Dog. Nevah did think you'd run out on youah family." Very gently his pliant fingers slipped up and down Sean's broken leg. Billy felt Sean's other wounds. "I know, Dog. You been fightin' somethin' that would have fought Penny. That's why you didn't stay heah when we came. You had to be away. But don't trouble youah head any mo'. We can fix you up. Let's get some wood lighted."

Sean followed contentedly behind when Billy gathered wood for their fire, and he lay down in the snow while Billy arranged it. He had run very hard, and he had fought very hard, and some decisions were just not for dogs to make. From now on Sean would always know exactly what to do because he would always know exactly what Billy wanted. The big Setter watched, fascinated, while Billy lighted the first fire that had warmed Sean since last summer.

Billy took some bannock and venison out of his pack sack and divided it exactly in half. Sean ate hungrily, knowing that sharing his master's food was a good dog's just due. The fire flared brighter. Billy's arm stole out to slide around Sean's neck, and the big Setter wriggled contentedly as he watched the fire.

Billy was watching the fire too, with the contentment of a mind made up. No longer was he undecided, or fearful, for certainly a man had to be at least as good as his dog. Sean, too, might have run from his enemy, his problem, but he hadn't. He had faced responsibility as best he could. Billy could do no less.

Sean limped beside him when Billy broke off small pine branches and laid them on the snow. He spread his blanket on them, and pushed a reflecting log into place. Both stretched out.

Not tonight, but tomorrow, they would make a very slow trip back to Billy's cabin. There Sean's broken leg could be splinted and given time to heal. After that . . .

"Yes, suh," Billy said softly. "Aftah that you and me will be goin' back to Danny Pickett's."

ABOUT THE AUTHOR

JIM KJELGAARD's first book was *Forest Patrol* (1941), based on the wilderness experiences of himself and his brother, a forest ranger. Since then he has written many others—all of them concerned with the out-of-doors. *Big Red, Irish Red,* and *Outlaw Red* are dog stories about Irish setters. *Kalak of the Ice* (a polar bear) and *Chip, the Dam Builder* (a beaver) are wild-animal stories. *Snow Dog* and *Wild Trek* describe the adventures of a trapper and his half-wild dog. *Haunt Fox* is the story both of a fox and of the dog and boy who trailed him, and *Stormy* is concerned with a wildfowl retriever and his young owner. *Fire-Hunter* is a story about prehistoric man; *Boomerang Hunter* about the equally primitive Australian aborigine. *Rebel Siege* and *Buckskin Brigade* are tales of American frontiersmen, and *Wolf Brother* presents the Indian side of "the winning of the West." The cougar-hunting *Lion Hound* and the greyhound story, *Desert Dog,* are laid in the present-day Southwest. *A Nose for Trouble* and *Trailing Trouble* are adventure mysteries centered around a game warden and his man-hunting bloodhound. The same game warden also appears in *Wildlife Cameraman* and *Hidden Trail,* stories about a young nature photographer and his dog.

JIM KJELGAARD

In these adventure stories, Jim Kjelgaard shows us the special world of animals, the wilderness, and the bonds between men and dogs. *Irish Red* and *Outlaw Red* are stories about two champion Irish setters. *Snow Dog* shows what happens when a half-wild dog crosses paths with a trapper. The cougar-hunting *Lion Hound* and the greyhound story *Desert Dog* take place in our present-day Southwest. And, *Stormy* is an extraordinary story of a boy and his devoted dog. You'll want to read all these exciting books.

☐	15578	A NOSE FOR TROUBLE	$2.75
☐	15547	HAUNT FOX	$2.50
☐	15434	BIG RED	$2.95
☐	15546	IRISH RED: SON OF BIG RED	$2.75
☐	15427	LION HOUND	$2.95
☐	15339	OUTLAW RED	$2.50
☐	15560	SNOW DOG	$2.95
☐	15468	STORMY	$2.95
☐	15466	WILD TREK	$2.75

Prices and availability subject to change without notice.

FROM THE SPOOKY, EERIE PEN OF JOHN BELLAIRS . . .

☐ **THE CURSE OF THE BLUE FIGURINE**　　15540/$2.95

Johnny Dixon knows a lot about ancient Egypt and curses and evil spirits—but when he finds the blue figurine, he actually "sees" a frightening, super-natural world. Even his friend Professor Childermass can't help him!

☐ **THE MUMMY, THE WILL AND THE CRYPT**　　15498/$2.75

For months Johnny has been working on a riddle that would lead to a $10,000 reward. Feeling certain that the money is hidden somewhere in the house of a dead man, Johnny goes into his house where a bolt of lightning reveals to him that the house is not quite deserted . . .

☐ **THE SPELL OF THE SORCERER'S SKULL**　　15579/$2.75

Johnny Dixon is back, but this time he's not teamed up with Dr. Childermass. That's because his friend, the Professor, has disappeared!

Shop at home
for quality children's books
and save money, too.

Now you can order books for the whole family from Bantam's latest catalog of hundreds of titles including many fine children's books. *And* this special offer gives you an opportunity to purchase a Bantam book for only 50¢. Here's how:

By ordering any five books at the regular price per order, you can also choose any other single book listed (up to a $5.95 value) for just 50¢. Some restrictions do apply, so for further details send for Bantam's catalog of titles today.